DATE DUE			

F
KRO
PB

Krossing, Karen.

The Yo-Yo Prophet

MOOSEHEART SCHOOL LIBRARY
MOOSEHEART, IL

629758 00897 12555C

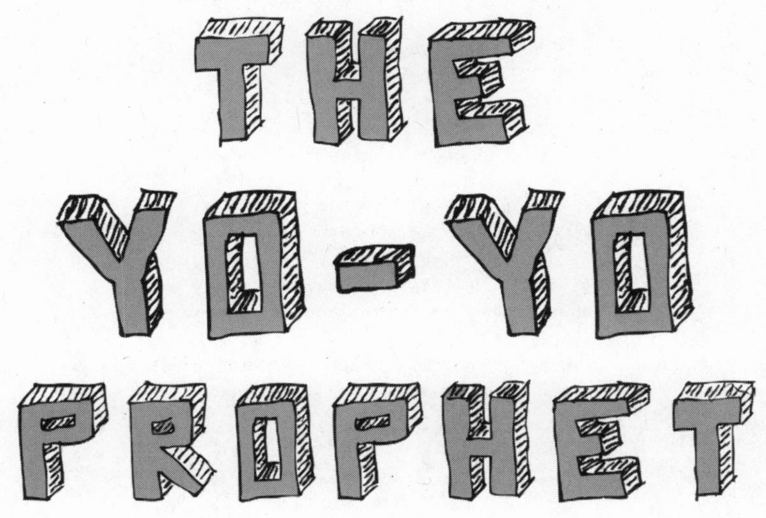

KAREN KROSSING

ORCA BOOK PUBLISHERS

Text copyright © 2011 Karen Krossing

All rights reserved. No part of this publication may be reproduced or transmitted in any form or by any means, electronic or mechanical, including photocopying, recording or by any information storage and retrieval system now known or to be invented, without permission in writing from the publisher.

Library and Archives Canada Cataloguing in Publication

Krossing, Karen, 1965-
The Yo-Yo Prophet / Karen Krossing.

Issued also in electronic format.
ISBN 978-1-55469-827-1

I. Title.
PS8571.R776Y6 2011 JC813'.6 C2011-903340-2

First published in the United States, 2011
Library of Congress Control Number: 2011907467

Summary: Small, shy Calvin becomes the Yo-Yo Prophet when his street tricks get the attention of a bully named Rozelle.

Orca Book Publishers is dedicated to preserving the environment and has printed this book on paper certified by the Forest Stewardship Council®.

Orca Book Publishers gratefully acknowledges the support for its publishing programs provided by the following agencies: the Government of Canada through the Canada Book Fund and the Canada Council for the Arts, and the Province of British Columbia through the BC Arts Council and the Book Publishing Tax Credit.

Cover design by Teresa Bubela
Cover photo by Getty Images

ORCA BOOK PUBLISHERS
PO Box 5626, Stn. B
Victoria, BC Canada
V8R 6S4

ORCA BOOK PUBLISHERS
PO Box 468
Custer, WA USA
98240-0468

www.orcabook.com
Printed and bound in Canada.

14 13 12 11 • 4 3 2 1

For Tess, Paige and Kevin

"Pull the string, and it will follow wherever you wish. Push it, and it will go nowhere at all."

—Dwight D. Eisenhower

After math class, I end up with my face planted in Rozelle's chest.

I don't know how it happens. One moment I'm shuffling between the desks, eager to get to my locker and escape. Head down, black high-tops scuffing the floor, binders tucked under one arm. Math class always leaves me feeling stupid.

"You'll know the answer to this problem, Calvin," my math teacher, Mr. Marnello, always says. As if I must be good at math because I'm half Asian.

I glance across the classroom to see Mr. Marnello gazing after me, shaking his head. His glasses slip down his nose, and his eyes are still quizzing me over the rims.

I cringe and lurch away. The next moment, I find my nose burrowed in Rozelle's floral-scented flesh.

I jerk free, shaking. My face is level with her cleavage. Rozelle looks nothing like she did when I met her back in grade three, when she beat up Marcus Ramsay, the biggest guy in our class, just to prove she could. My eyes dart nervously from one magnificent boob to the other before they rise to meet her glare.

"Little Calvin Layne." Rozelle sneers, her teeth white against dark skin. "What the hell you think you're doin'?"

Her posse gathers around, shielding me from Mr. Marnello. Rozelle shoves me into the hall, her beefy arms jingling with bracelets.

My cheeks burn, making my eyes water. "I didn't mean..." My voice fails.

"Whoa, Roz! I do believe you're gonna make this boy cry." Sasha, who is Rozelle's number one, pretends to sob.

"He's too small to bother with." Annette, Rozelle's number two, giggles. Her hand rises to her burgundy-painted lips. "He's the smallest guy in grade nine!"

"Yeah, he's Low-Cal." Sasha grins.

My shoulders sink.

"Hardly a mouthful." Rozelle snorts.

"Not worth a taste." Sasha nudges her.

Rozelle throws back her head, hooting. "You're right, girls. I need somethin'"—she pauses—"meatier."

Her posse cackles. Sasha slaps Rozelle on the back. Annette collapses against a locker, laughing.

I attempt to run, but Sasha blocks my escape. Rozelle's breath flames the back of my neck. Her fist closes around my puny bicep.

"Remember this, Low-Cal," she says. "I ain't bustin' you. So you owe me."

When she releases me, I burst through the tangle of polished brown arms and legs. Brush against fabric that's silky to the touch. Flee the perfume that makes my head ache.

Minutes later, I erupt from the school, backpack sliding off one shoulder. A hot breeze assaults me. It feels muggy and thick, like it's summer already, even though it's only May. I weave around a knot of grade twelves, not slowing until I reach the sidewalk, shaded by overhanging trees.

"Calvin!" I hear Geordie call from somewhere behind me. Geordie, who sits beside me in science, is obsessed with superheroes.

I'm beside the bus stop now, where two guys in black leather jackets stand on the concrete bench like they own it. Guys who like to mock geeks who talk about superheroes.

I take off toward the subway, pretending I don't hear Geordie. My arm feels bruised, the back of my neck raw. After my encounter with Rozelle, I want to stay off the radar. Fly low to the ground.

I slouch on the subway seat until I get to my stop, and then I hike up the stairs to blink in the sunlight. At a busy street corner, I stop with the crowd, waiting for the traffic lights to change. My hand slips into my pocket, and I clutch the lightweight butterfly yo-yo I find there.

Tired two-story shops line the streets; they look like they're trying to prop each other up. Across the street and twelve doors down is home: the cramped apartment above Queen's Dry Cleaning, named for Gran's love of British royalty. I can see the blue-and-white-striped awning from where I stand. There's a cheesy poster of a young Queen Elizabeth II in the window.

It will be stifling in there. Skunky. It always is, till hours after the shop has closed and the equipment has cooled. And Gran will be either giving back too many coins or shortchanging the customers. How does a person who's run a shop for over forty years suddenly forget how to make change?

I pull back from the crowd at the corner. I don't want to deal with Gran yet. I'm not ready to hear her call me the wrong name, or listen to her watery cough. I feel like an elastic band that's pulled too tight.

With my shoulders against the sun-warmed bricks of the bank, I pull the yo-yo from my pocket, cupping it in my palm. People like Rozelle would call it a toy and make fun of me forever, but the street-corner crowd won't care what I do.

I loop the string around my middle finger before throwing the yo-yo. I put it to sleep—spinning it in place at the end of the uncoiled string—and then toss a few power throws. My mind whirls with the yo-yo, unraveling my thoughts.

The traffic lights change, and the crowd surges on without me, jostling against the people heading the opposite way. A car horn sounds as the driver tries to edge through the throng to turn the corner. At the curb, a cube van belches out diesel fumes, its engine rumbling.

Moving out from the wall, I can't resist tossing a few simple tricks—rock the baby, elevator, tidal wave. My hands whir, my arms loosen up. I've only practiced at home, but this feels pretty fine. I take up more of the sidewalk. People weave around me, staying clear of the yo-yo as it extends and then glides back. There's only me and the yo-yo, working with the noise and confusion of the street corner.

A new crowd is forming at the lights, waiting to cross. I make the yo-yo hover like a flying saucer.

"Nice trick," one guy says.

A little girl with tight braids stares at me until the Walk signal blinks and her mother yanks her away.

Grinning, I throw a breakaway loop to the right, letting the yo-yo circle down and across to the left. I loop the string up and over the index finger of my left hand and flip the yo-yo to trapeze across the horizontal string.

I'm in the zone. The crowd and the street are vanishing, leaving a calm circle of light and heat around me. The yo-yo dances at the end of the string, spins back into my hand and then releases again. It's a dream. A happy one.

"Hey!"

A man's voice. I look up, my yo-yo still spinning.

A balding man in a dark blue suit heads toward me. He extends one hand, fingers closed around something. "Here you go, kid."

My right hand is still working the yo-yo. No time to think. My left hand flashes out, palm open.

The balding man unloads a handful of change. I close my fist around it. What the hell? I tug my yo-yo home. The man steps off the curb into the street.

"Thanks!" I call.

The man turns and smiles before he disappears into the crowd.

A week later, I'm shoving a pile of comic books off my bed and arranging my yo-yo collection across my faded *Star Wars* sheets. Which yo-yo should I choose?

As the shadows lengthen outside my window, I try out my favorites, one by one. My first ever—a wooden yo-yo I got in a loot bag when I was six. Chipped and horribly unbalanced. No good for performing, but I'll never get rid of it.

My butterfly yo-yo is great for string tricks. Metallic purple. Hard-core quality. Too small though. A crowd wouldn't be able to see it.

I test a red yo-yo with a classic shape. It's larger, brighter, excellent for looping tricks.

But my neon-yellow yo-yo catches my eye. Brilliant color. As big as my fist. Shaped for both string and looping tricks. It feels steady in my hand. Comfortable. Impressive, I hope. Will it be enough?

The idea has haunted me for days—ever since that man on the street corner gave me a handful of coins. Could I perform on the street for money? Would people actually pay? Would they even stop to watch?

Over and over I've relived the scene. The guy who admired my flying-saucer trick. The girl who stared at me. Best of all—the man who gave me the coins. I guess he thought I was a street performer.

My fingers tighten around the neon yo-yo. I could do even better. Earn enough for a new yo-yo. Maybe a Silver Bullet. I've always wanted one, but they're expensive.

As Gran's snores begin to drift from her room, I head down to the shop to power up her ancient computer, leaving the lights off and the blinds slanted shut.

Surrounded by rows of neatly hung clothes trapped in plastic bags, I download videos of world championship yo-yo routines, studying the moves. When I watch a little kid who can out-perform me, my stomach twists. Will people laugh at me? What am I thinking?

I have to create a routine I can't mess up. No difficult tricks, just ones that will amaze people long enough to make them stop and watch. People who usually take one look at me and think I'm too small, too young, to do anything really cool.

The chemical scent in the shop gives me a headache. My eyes get sore. I lower my head onto my arms and close my eyes, just for a minute. I fall asleep over the keyboard and dream of performing to a jeering crowd.

I wake with an aching neck and the imprint of the keyboard on my cheek. Overhead, the floorboards creak with Gran's footsteps. The sun is peeking through the blinds, trapping dust in its beams.

I groan and stretch. Then I turn off the computer and hurry upstairs to dress. As I brush my teeth and flatten my spiky hair, a series of tricks begins to form in my mind. A double or nothing. And I'll do reach-for-the-moon. That will be good for a crowd. I can imagine that Silver Bullet in my palm already.

At school, I avoid Rozelle and her gang as much as possible. I sit in the front row in math and science, the two classes I have with them, and I eat in the cafeteria, a place they'd never be caught dead. I hope they've moved on to fresh targets. I hope Rozelle's forgotten me.

At home I practice my tricks in the living room, performing for the royal faces on Gran's collection of souvenir plates, teacups, mugs and saucers. Mounted on walls and cluttering the tabletops, the hand-painted china makes me jittery, but my room is too small for looping tricks. I haven't broken any of Gran's stuff yet.

When I get too hot—and too worried about crashing a yo-yo into royalty—I move to the alley behind the store. The smell of rotting food drifts from the Dumpster, and the laneway is coated with grease from the diner next door.

Van sits out back on an old kitchen chair, taking a break from the shop. She's second in command after Gran, and I know that for the last few months she's held the shop, and Gran, together.

Van claps after every trick. Her cheeks dimple. "Your *bà* must be so proud!"

I shrug. "I haven't shown Gran."

Van was my mother's childhood friend in Vietnam. She's as soft on me as I imagine my mother would be. Even when my yo-yo spins out of control, snaps its string and whacks against the Dumpster, Van praises me.

"I only hope my new grandchild will be as fine as you!" Van smiles. Her daughter, who lives in Vancouver, is about to have another baby. Van is young for a grandmother, way younger than Gran.

"Thanks, Van." I examine my yo-yo for cracks, frowning.

Van heads inside. "See you later," she says in Vietnamese, even though I hardly understand the language.

When I'm sure my yo-yo isn't broken, I head up the back stairs, brooding. Van makes me feel good—almost like my mother did—but she's a lousy audience. I need a tougher sell to see if I'm good enough to take it to the streets.

As I restring my yo-yo, I think about showing my routine to Geordie. I met Geordie back in September when we started grade nine. He's pretty much my only friend, since most of the people I knew in middle school are too cool to talk to me now. They go to ravine parties that I'm not invited to and talk about who wants to hook up. Since no one's asking to hook up with either of us, Geordie and I hang out together, mostly at lunch. Geordie is really tall, pimpled and crazy about his comic collection. He fits in about as well as I do. If I show him my routine, maybe he won't laugh.

I bring my yo-yo to school three days in a row before I even try to show Geordie. What if Rozelle sees me yo-yoing? What will she do to me then?

I convince Geordie to eat lunch behind the portables because it's out of the way. He paces across the strip of weedy grass between a portable and the parking lot, talking about which superhero has the coolest powers.

"I mean, I wouldn't mind superstrength or mind control." Geordie speaks slowly, like he has to chew each word before he says it. He hunches his shoulders, which doesn't make him look any shorter, and his oversize T-shirt hangs over his skinny chest. "Flying is all right, but you can't fight anyone with it."

I grip the yo-yo in my pocket, willing myself to say it: *Check this out*. Then I'll launch into my routine, and Geordie will fall over in shock. I've never shown anyone at school what I can do.

But my hands tremble so much that I know I'll fail.

It has to be Gran. She'll be my practice audience.

•••

I approach Gran in the shop late Saturday night, after Van and the others have gone home. She's bent over a sewing machine, wearing blue jeans and a pink T-shirt. Her pale skin and white hair give off a ghostly glow under the glare of her table lamp. Tall and heavyset, with blue eyes and a slight mustache, Gran looks nothing like me. With my Vietnamese features, it's like I'm not related to her.

"Must be something wrong with the bobbin, Your Majesty," Gran says. She opens a door in the side of the machine and pulls out a silver bobbin, tangled with thread. She tugs at the thread to unravel it, pausing when a cough overtakes her.

I cringe at the sound of her cough. "Gran?"

"Give me a minute, Richard."

"It's me—Calvin." I sigh. "Dad's not here, remember?"

"I'm just finishing up with Her Majesty."

I grit my teeth, wondering who she's talking to. I remember when her thoughts were clear. When she could answer all the questions on *Jeopardy*—her favorite game show—before the contestants did. When she'd tell me stories about my father getting into trouble around the shop as a kid. He almost suffocated in a plastic dry-cleaning bag when he curled up inside, pretending to be a goldfish in a bowl. Gran also told me how my parents met when she hired my mother. How my father asked my mother out every day until she said yes.

I moved in with Gran six years ago, after my mother died and my dad disappeared to "run the bases," as Gran called it. "He's wandering the world, looking for a place to belong, forgetting that he belongs right here with us," she used to say.

Now, her mind sometimes gets cloudy and her watery cough never goes away. Not that she's old. Only sixty-eight. But she seems much older.

My chest hurts when I remember how she used to be. Only a few months ago, she could finish the newspaper Sudoku in half an hour. She managed the shop as if she were the Queen of England and still had the energy to go to flea markets on Sundays, looking for more royal china to add to her collection.

"Mr. Spider wants to buy it, Your Majesty," Gran rambles on, as she replaces the bobbin in the machine. "I finally found a purchaser. After all this time."

"Mr. Spider?" I touch Gran's rounded shoulder. "Gran, what are you talking about?"

Gran pats my hand absentmindedly. Her skin is dry and loose, like it's too big for her bones. "I did it for you."

"Did what, Gran?"

Gran swivels in her chair. Her crinkly eyes find mine. "Sold to Mr. Spider, of course."

There she goes again, I think.

"Gran, I need to talk to you," I begin. "Listen." I wait as she slides her glasses to the tip of her nose and her eyes seem clearly focused on my face. Then I tell her everything: how I earned money doing yo-yo tricks on the street when I wasn't even trying, how I practiced a routine of string and looping tricks with my best yo-yo, how I need someone to tell me if my routine is good. I even tell her how terrified I am that I'll fail.

Gran watches my routine three times, frowning when I miss a trick and nodding when I succeed.

"Not bad," she says. She goes to the cash register, opens it and offers me a five-dollar bill.

I refuse it. "Do you think I should do it?"

"You'll be great, Richard."

I turn away, my eyes burning. Just when I think she may be getting better, she gets confused again. A lot of the time now, she has no clue who I am. Gran can't help me. Still, I have to try street performing. I need to chase that rush one more time. Even if I fail. Even if they laugh me off the street.

On Monday in science class, I trip over Geordie's backpack, stumble and hit the floor with my hands raised to break my fall. My legs are splayed across the aisle between the desks. Shock waves pulse through my arms and chest, and I gasp for air, inhaling dust and the scent of industrial floor polish.

The laughter starts with a muffled snort from the back of the classroom. Whispers and giggles spread as fast as a computer virus. My face heats up.

"Sorry, Calvin," Geordie mumbles. "You okay?"

Geordie's size-twelve basketball shoes appear beside my head, but I can only blink. The yo-yos in the pockets of my hoodie press into my gut.

"Get up, Mr. Layne," calls my science teacher, Ms. Kinsela. "We have bean plants to measure."

I groan and push off the floor. Twenty-nine sets of eyes are on me. Potted bean plants sit ignored on the desks. Geordie towers over me, making me feel puny. I duck my head, but I can't avoid the weight of all those eyes.

My hoodie hangs slack off one shoulder. As I yank it back in place, the neon yo-yo spills from my pocket. It clatters across the floor and twirls to a stop three desks back—at Rozelle's feet.

I freeze.

Rozelle rests an elbow on the desk she shares with Sasha. She glances down at the yo-yo and raises one eyebrow, her dark eyes measuring mine. "You sendin' me a gift, Low-Cal?"

"Uh..." A shiver of panic crawls up my back. Will she tease me about playing with a toy? Pretend it's not yours, I think. But then I'd never get it back.

Sasha smirks. "Maybe he likes you."

My eyes dart away and back again. I'm sure my face can't get any redder.

"All right." Ms. Kinsela raises her head from her marking. "You should be recording your observations in your growth chart now."

I head toward my seat, shoving my second yo-yo and spare string deeper into my pocket. Ms. Kinsela has a drawer full of stuff she's taken from students. Did she see my yo-yo go flying? Will she take it? Will Rozelle?

I have to rescue it.

When Ms. Kinsela returns to her marking, I scoot down the aisle, my body awkward, like I'm just learning to walk.

Rozelle is whispering to Sasha, and as I get closer I can hear what she's saying. "So I told my brother he's gotta learn the music business. You know, get his name out there. He's got a sweet sound. He could be frickin' huge."

Avoiding eye contact, I try to casually crawl under Rozelle's desk as if it's something I do every day. My neon yo-yo rests beside Rozelle's black combat boots; her chunky legs are barely contained by a jean miniskirt. I tremble. This is territory I never expected to encounter.

"Calvin! Get out! Ms. Kinsela!" Sasha lets out a phony scream; she can't possibly be afraid of me. I jump, whacking my head on the underside of the desk.

My head throbs. I reach toward my yo-yo. Rozelle's chair slides back, and her face appears under the table.

"Are you peepin'?" She sneers. "Teacher's not gonna like that."

I cringe. Peep at Rozelle? Never. My chest is pounding. I grab my yo-yo before Rozelle can snatch it, and then I shimmy backward, out from under the desk.

Ms. Kinsela is waiting in the aisle, her arms crossed over her lab coat, one heel tapping.

"I'll see you for detention, Mr. Layne."

I leap up, swallowing the wave of acid burning my throat. I nod at Ms. Kinsela and pray that Rozelle won't point out the yo-yo behind my back.

"Did you see him, Ms. Kinsela?" Rozelle fakes a wounded voice. "He tried to look up my skirt!"

I stand rigid, hands clammy with sweat.

Sasha joins in, ever faithful to her leader. "He was right underneath us! What did he think he was doing?"

I flush again. It's too much humiliation.

"Enough, girls." Ms. Kinsela silences Sasha. "I'll address the situation after school."

"But I feel so vi-o-la-ted," Rozelle says, drawing out each syllable. "Maybe he should be suspended."

"I said that's enough, Miss Jones. Now get back to work. All of you." Ms. Kinsela stares pointedly at me.

I scurry to my desk and drop into my chair. I slip my yo-yo back into my pocket, wipe my hands dry on my shorts and hunch over the desk, wanting to disappear.

So what if Rozelle knows I have a yo-yo? Maybe no one else saw. Maybe no one will care.

Geordie slouches into the chair beside mine, folding his legs under the desk. "Was that a yo-yo?" he whispers.

"Um, yeah." I stiffen. "But it's not mine."

"Then why is it in your pocket?"

I glance down at my pathetic bean plant. Its brown leaves are withered, and a dank smell of rot rises from it. Geordie's long, lush plant winds around its bamboo stake.

"It's for…my cousin." As if I have anyone other than Gran.

Geordie nods. He ducks his head as Ms. Kinsela marches to the front of the room.

Does he believe me? I'll never know because Ms. Kinsela is surveying her domain, forcing our conversation to end.

I pick up my ruler and begin measuring my scrawny plant. I have to be smart. Smarter than everyone else. Smarter than Rozelle. That can't be so hard, can it?

•••

I can't figure out where to put my hat.

It's a blue baseball cap with a black brim. An old hat I don't care about. When I sit it upside down on the brick path, it looks like the wind tossed it there. No one will drop a coin in it.

I'm at Mason Parkette, a triangular thoroughfare to the subway with a line of shops on one side. I scan the parkette for a better place to set up: the walkways crowded with people, the weedy patches of grass, the scattered benches.

A few spindly trees struggle to grow in large block planters. A low circular fountain glitters with pennies—wishes that might never come true. I resist the urge to toss my own penny in the fountain, like I used to do when Mom was sick. Instead, I find an empty stone bench near the row of shops: Athena Travel Service, Lucky Convenience, Hillier's Jewelry, Iron Kettle Pub. The bench is an island on a concrete pad. A perfect place for my crowd to gather. If they gather.

I drop my hat on the bench. It's upside down, ready for coins. I dig in my backpack for my yo-yos, which I tucked safely away before detention. First, Ms. Kinsela lectured me about respect, and then she made me write lines for an hour. At least no one was around to humiliate me when I left.

I pull out my neon yo-yo and my spare, just in case. I unzip my hoodie and toss it and my backpack under the bench. Then I stand on the bench and begin to warm up with a few forward passes.

I launch into some large looping tricks to attract attention: around-the-world forward and backward. I'm distracted by trying to figure out if anyone's watching me, so my loops are wobbly and weak.

Pigeons strut around the bench, pecking at the seeds someone tossed there. A mother pushing a baby in a stroller ignores me. A kid practices skateboarding off another bench. Three old men sitting near the fountain shout at each other in what I think is Italian. They sound like they're arguing, but they might just be talking about their favorite soccer teams.

The pigeons are my only audience.

Should I give up before I embarrass myself? I whir through a few more lame tricks and then launch into my routine even though I'm shaking and unsteady. I begin with a breakaway loop leading to a double or nothing, which I barely manage. I try to throw a three-leaf clover, but I give up mid-trick.

My tricks are rocky. I need to calm down. I break from my routine to throw as many loop-the-loops as I can. Three. Five. Seven. My brain begins to untangle. My shoulders loosen. Thoughts of how stupid I look unwind and spin off in all directions. When the yo-yo slows, I tug it home and begin a fresh series of loops.

When I feel stronger, I do ten reach-for-the-moons. Perfectly. My body's starting to hum along with the yo-yo. I'm doing it, and people are coming to watch. I steal glimpses at the skateboarder, his board tucked under one arm; the mother with the stroller, the baby sucking her thumb and following the yo-yo with her eyes; a group of kids who are maybe eleven years old; a man smoking a cigarette. All watching me. And no pigeons in sight.

I'm smooth. In the groove. I walk-the-dog, letting the yo-yo run along the bench like a dog on a leash. I throw another sleeper, bringing the dog behind my legs to walk through them. I put my yo-yo hand on my hip. I would say, "Jump through the hoop, Rover," but I don't want to jinx myself by trying to talk. I tug the yo-yo to make it leap up from behind and through the hoop made by my arm.

"Cool!" one kid says. "Do it again."

I smile. Warmth fills my chest. My hands guide the yo-yo through the tricks. I'm a lion tamer dominating a wild beast. It's awesome. Powerful.

I think I see Rozelle in the growing crowd. My hands tense and I miss a trick, although no one seems to notice. I stare again between tosses. Catch a glimpse of her behind a tall man with wide shoulders. She's turned away, ignoring my show. If it's her. Why would she be here? As if she'd follow me.

I have to relax. It can't be her. I focus only on the yo-yo spinning at the end of the string. I make the shape of the Eiffel Tower and follow it with a bow tie. My audience applauds.

I finish my routine and launch into it again. I'm not ready for this to end. I feel like I'm floating, my feet levitating off the bench. I'm not Calvin Layne anymore, but someone new, someone bigger. Better.

As I work my tricks, the crowd yells its approval, goes silent and then bursts to life again. I begin to think of them as one unit, one living creature that moves together, claps together, breathes together. When a single voice from the crowd speaks out, I'm surprised.

"Go away! Get out of here!"

Outside Hillier's Jewelry, a short man in a sweater vest is making shooing motions with his hands. He's wearing tiny metal-frame glasses and a scowl.

I ignore him. Maybe he'll leave. I perform a hop-the-fence trick, where the yo-yo jumps over my hand.

"Did you hear me, boy?" the man yells. "It's hard enough to earn a living without riffraff hanging around outside my store."

Riffraff? What am I—some kind of criminal?

I throw some loop-the-loops and glance around. Maybe ten or more people stand in front of Hillier's Jewelry. They fill most of the space, except for a wide circle around the glaring man.

I think of Gran, trying to make money in her shop. She wouldn't mind if I performed outside Queen's Dry Cleaning. Maybe it would bring her more customers.

"I'm not doing anything wrong, sir." I'm pumped, not ready to quit. I whirl into another trick.

The man's still yelling. "I was robbed twice last month. I know how you street punks operate."

Street punk? My jaw tightens. I have as much right to be here as he does.

"Are you here to case out my store?" the man continues. "Or maybe you're the lookout? Well, I'm not giving you the chance. Go on now!"

"Don't go! We want more yo!" someone yells.

I get an injection of energy. These people love me. Me! "I'm a performer, not a thief," I tell the man.

The crowd shouts its approval.

"And if you yelled like that, you'd scare off any thieves," I say.

A few people laugh. The man's face reddens. His eyes bulge out. He's going to blow.

Maybe I went too far. "I meant that when—uh, if—some guys try to rob you, you would be tough enough to get rid of them. You're..." The man's face is deep crimson. Time to clear out—before he calls the cops. "I'll be gone in a minute."

He shakes a fist at me. "You'd better be."

I take a breath before my final trick. I throw a hard sleeper and then carefully remove the loop of string around my middle finger. I call the yo-yo back up with a tug on the string and just before it reaches my hand, I jerk the string up and let go, string and all. The yo-yo skyrockets into the air. The crowd cheers, and I'm defying gravity again. I grab my hat, catching the yo-yo in it on the way back down.

"Thanks!" I wave my hat in the air and then place it back on the bench, hoping to attract contributions. Not that I need the money. The cheering is enough. "Come back next week." I add, without thinking. I'd love to work this crowd forever.

"Not in front of my shop!" the jewelry store owner yells.

"No, over there." I point toward the fountain.

Several people shout their approval. Others drop coins in my hat.

The man huffs away, back to his shop.

When I step down from the bench, I'm surrounded.

"That was awesome!"

"How'd you do it?"

"Where did you get that yo-yo?"

"What kind is it?"

One boy asks me to sign his forehead with black marker. Another wants to try my yo-yo.

When the crowd has finally left, I'm still buzzing. I pack away my yo-yos and hoodie. Turn when I feel eyes on my back. Another fan?

Rozelle. She's watching me from across the parkette. My stomach clenches. She smiles and then meanders toward me. The new, stronger Calvin Layne thuds back down to earth.

"Thought you were up to somethin." Rozelle's eyes are outlined by hard black lines with deep purple shadow on her eyelids. Her skin-tight top and faded blue jeans reveal every bulge, every curve. I tear my eyes away.

"Uh..." I struggle to find some hard words to shoot at her.

"You could do better though." She nods, making her huge hoop earrings wobble. "Looks like you need a manager, Low-Cal."

"Wha-at?" The word sticks to the roof of my mouth.

Rozelle eyes my hat, heavy with coins and even a few bills. "I could do it for fifty percent." She scoops about half my earnings out of my hat.

"But...that's mine!" My hand comes to life. Jerks the hat away from her.

Rozelle grimaces and leans in. She cracks her peppermint gum like it's some kind of threat.

I cringe, waiting for the blow to fall. Rozelle has been beating guys up since grade three, although she's never bothered with me before.

Her grimace twists into a half smile, lips closed. "Listen, I got a personal interest here." She looks down and away, like she's embarrassed, and I wonder if she's faking it and why.

"What are you talking about?"

"I gotta show my brother I can be a good manager." Her tough face reappears. "Not that it's any of your business. And if you go tellin' anyone, I'll..." Her hands become fists, but she keeps them at her sides.

I step back. I can't imagine what her brother must be like. Or the rest of her family. "I don't know—"

"We can make a lot of money together." She smiles and steps closer. Her fists relax. "I'll be a frickin' awesome manager. I'll make you famous. Anyway, you owe me for what you did in math class. Remember how you slammed into my boobs? Almost knocked me over? That was harsh. But you can make it up to me now." She grabs my hand and shakes it like we just made a deal.

Her touch sends an electric shock through me. Her hand is surprisingly warm, firm and strong. I nod dumbly and immediately regret it.

"Cool." Rozelle grins. "I'll start makin' plans. Be in touch soon." She releases my hand and saunters away.

I watch her hips sway. They're hypnotizing. My hand is still warm. My blood is pumping fast.

What have I done?

She disappears around the corner of the Iron Kettle Pub. I collapse onto the bench, clenching my hat full of money between white-knuckled fingers.

"Hey, Peeper! Roz's looking for you." Sasha is posed beside Annette's locker like a skinny praying mantis about to pounce. "She wants to talk."

Annette smirks at me as she slams her locker closed. I pick up the pace, head down and jaw clenched, racing for the exit doors—and freedom—pretending I don't hear.

"Where you going?" Sasha calls.

"I think he's going to spy on the girls in the change room." Annette giggles and Sasha joins in.

The metal door clangs shut behind me, but the laughter still burns my ears.

When the door opens again, I'm already scurrying away like the bug I am.

"Roz isn't going to like this!" Sasha calls from the doorway.

I race down the sidewalk and past the entrance to the subway, nails digging into my palms. Today I need to walk. I don't care if it takes hours to get home. I want time to think about how to get rid of Rozelle.

Thanks to her, the last three days have been hell. I've been skulking around the school, never sure when she'll pin me down, try to make plans for my next show. I had to dart into washrooms to avoid her girls, and duck her double-barreled stare in classes.

At least it's almost June. After school is over, I'll be free of them—for a while.

I slow down, in no hurry to get home, and clomp past rows of townhouses with wrought-iron gates and tiny yards. I hit a main street, still fuming. Why did I let her take my money? Why did I shake her hand? What exactly does she think I agreed to? Rozelle is a thief. A liar. A bully. I don't want anything to do with her.

I pass a homeless shelter, the front stairs crowded with sprawling men. Then a tattoo parlor, a Thai restaurant, a Greek bakery with the door open—the smell of pastry and honey wafting out to tempt me.

My mouth waters, but I've brought none of my hard-earned cash, half of which Rozelle stole. I grind my teeth, wishing I hadn't told my yo-yo crowd when and where I'd be back. Will they expect me to keep my word? What if I find a new place to perform, away from Rozelle? But I want to go back. I want to feel that good again. And she'll probably hunt me down no matter where I go. So I have to do it. I have to tell Rozelle that I don't want a manager.

My stomach lurches. Impossible. I step into the street to avoid a dog walker with a pack of dogs. Rozelle will probably clobber me and then do whatever she wants anyway.

My hands become jittery. I pull a yo-yo from my bag and begin to toss it. I strike a rhythm, throwing a forward pass every other step. The string tightens around my finger; the yo-yo smacks against my palm. With or without Rozelle, I have to make a new routine. My show has to be different than before, better somehow. Should I learn a new set of tricks? Or use the same ones in a different order? How can I keep my show fresh?

A new yo-yo? Or maybe two. I can learn two-handed tricks. That will bring the crowds.

I pick up my pace, tossing every three steps now. I'll order two new yo-yos online. Silver Bullets are too much, but I'll find two cheaper ones that are the same weight and color. I'll have to ask Gran to use her credit card to order them. After all, I can pay her back. I have cash now, even if Rozelle stole half of it.

•••

When I get home, I can hear Gran chatting in the living room, probably talking to her collection of plates. I kick off my shoes, frowning.

Another voice makes me strain to hear more. A man's voice. No man has set foot in the apartment since the last time my father visited, maybe three years ago.

My chest tightens. It couldn't be him. Could it? I hurry down the narrow hall and burst into the living room, colliding with a Charles-and-Diana wedding teapot on a side table. I catch the teapot before it falls off the table. Then I spin around to see Gran in her wingback armchair across from a tall pale man seated on the couch, a neat triangle of stubble on his chin.

Not my father. My gut twists. I get a flash of my father six years ago, stony-faced at my mother's funeral. He had always traveled a lot for work, designing the lights for music concerts. But after my mother died he left me with Gran and came home less and less often. After a while, we hardly saw him and didn't even know which city he was in. I flinch. Too much in one day. I want to crash into bed and pull my pillow over my head. Instead, I force a smile onto my face.

"Gran?" I glance back and forth between her and the man on the couch.

Gran looks lumpy in her sacklike blue dress. The man is stick-thin in skinny jeans, pointed black shoes and a purple collared shirt. When he stands, his head almost touches the ceiling light.

"This must be Calvin." He extends a bony hand, swallowing mine in his firm grip.

Who is this guy?

"Calvin, this is Mr. Spider," Gran says.

"Spider?" I feel like I've been slapped. Is this who Gran has been talking about? He's real? Maybe she isn't as far gone as I thought.

"Actually, my name is David Spader," the man is saying. "Most people just call me Spader, although your grandmother is determined to rename me."

"I've just been showing Mr. Spider the apartment, dear," Gran says.

"Gran, his name is Spader."

"Your grandmother can call me whatever she wants." Spader stands with his shoulders back, arms loose, one leg forward—like Gran's Prince Philip figurine. "I'm just glad we made a deal." He settles onto the couch.

"A deal?"

"I sold the building to Mr. Spider." Gran waves at the official-looking documents sitting on the coffee table between half-empty cups of tea. "Didn't I tell you?"

"What?" My jaw drops. "But...why? Where will we live?"

"Well, I'm not sure I've got all the details straight..." Gran begins to cough, hunching over, one hand covering her mouth and the other fluttering to her chest. Her face reddens.

"Gran!" I reach for her, but she motions me back. How can she not know where we're going to live?

"I'm...okay." She breathes heavily. "Really."

Spader clears his throat. "If I may explain?" He glances at Gran, who gives him a royal nod of assent.

I narrow my eyes at Spader, who smiles pleasantly. What is this guy up to?

"Your grandmother approached me a few months ago, offering to sell Queen's Dry Cleaning. She'd heard from a mutual business acquaintance that I wanted to start an eco business with an established customer base."

I stare at Gran. "Is this true?"

Gran nods, sips some tea and fans herself.

Spader continues. "After researching the potential of eco dry cleaning, I agreed to the purchase, and we signed the deal on May first. I'll take ownership of the building and Queen's Dry Cleaning in three weeks—on June seventeenth. You'll stay in the apartment above the store until August first. Your grandmother has told me that she prefers to find a new place to live, starting in August."

Why would he want to buy this place? I don't trust him. He's probably trying to swindle Gran. I turn to Gran, not caring if I sound rude. "You don't have to sell." She seems clearheaded right now, but does she really understand what she's doing?

"But I do, Calvin. I've been planning it for a long time, although I couldn't find a buyer—until now." She smiles at Spader like he's doing her a favor. "Things have to change. I'm not as young as I used to be. And I don't want to leave you with more than you can handle."

"Leave me? What are you talking about?"

"Oh, I just mean that I'm ready to retire. I can't keep up with things like I used to, Richard."

I wince.

Gran coughs, swallows hard and says to Spader, "Oh, there's one thing I've been meaning to talk to you about. Are you going to change the name of my shop? Because I am rather partial to it."

"Queen's Dry Cleaning? I can live with that."

Spader's smile matches the one that Prince Charles wears on his wedding teapot. Insincere. My stomach twists. I can't listen another minute. I have to get out of there. The dust gathering on the royal faces, the sound of traffic through the closed windows, the sun burning through the curtains, the smell of chemicals seeping up from downstairs. They all stifle me.

Without a word, I flee the apartment and end up pacing the back alley.

The contents of the Dumpster are festering in the heat, and the grease on the asphalt is as slick as Spader's smile. What if he turns out to be a crook? Con artists like to prey on old people, especially sick ones. I want Gran to have a nice retirement, but we could end up homeless and broke. I kick the Dumpster so hard that I slip and fall backward. I stumble to my feet, my arms, legs and clothes smeared with oil.

I want to scream. To throw things. Everything's going wrong. I want Rozelle off my back. I want Gran to get better. And I want Spader to leave us alone.

Then I notice the silence. The back door to the shop is propped open, yet the familiar hiss of the machines is missing. I step into the shop and listen.

Van and the other workers—Lucy and Franco—are huddled together, talking. I've never seen the shop so still, unless it was after hours.

"So you've heard?" I ask.

All eyes settle on me. Van takes in my grease stains and shakes her head. "Oh, Calvin. You need to get cleaned up."

Lucy and Franco slip away, the conversation abruptly over. As the hiss of machines starts up again, Van insists I wash up at the large industrial sink.

"Van, what's going to happen?" I turn on the water.

"I don't know," she says in Vietnamese, assuming I'll understand. She tries to wipe at my arm with a warm cloth, but I take it from her. "I suppose Mr. Spader will take over Queen's Dry Cleaning."

"Spader is a creep," I say, scrubbing my arms harder than I need to.

Van shakes her head. "No, he is a businessman."

I snort. "But is he honest? Who knows what kind of deal he made her sign?" I try to wipe the grease off my legs, but it just smears. "Did you read it?"

"I cannot read English legal papers so well, but your *bà* hired a lawyer to look it over. You know, she was lucky to find Mr. Spader."

"I hope so." I glance up. "Anyway, you'll still work here, right, Van? You'll be around to help Gran and me?"

Van's eyes slide sideways. She says something in Vietnamese that I don't understand. Then she adds, "I will always try to help you and your *bà*."

The bell jangles as someone enters the shop.

Van tries to pat me dry, but I take the towel from her.

“I’ll get it,” I say. There’s no use talking to Van about Spader. I need to keep busy so I won’t think about him.

I push through the rows of plastic-sheeted clothes to the front counter. The light from the window blinds me for a moment. I squint at the outline of a person as I inhale a whiff of familiar perfume.

No. It can’t be.

“You’ve been avoidin’ me, Low-Cal.” Rozelle glowers.

“What are you doing here?” I’m painfully aware of the grease stains on my clothes. “Do you follow me everywhere?” My hands tense. I’ve never wanted to hit anyone until today.

Rozelle leans on the long counter between us. “What’d you say?” Her tone is dangerous.

“I…uh…” Her biceps are bigger than my thighs. My hands turn to rubber.

“That’s better,” Rozelle says. “Now, I’ve been tryin’ to talk to you for frickin’ days.” She shakes her head, looking disappointed. “That’s not cool, Low-Cal. I had to ask ’round to find out where you live.”

“What do you want?” I say.

“I’m your manager, right? I wanna do a little managin’.”

Outside, Sasha and Annette pace the sidewalk, waiting for their leader to return. As I glare, Sasha fixes me with a stare. I look away. “I don’t need managing.”

My big moment—standing up to Rozelle. Pathetic.

"Trust me. You do. Here." She tosses me a shirt.

"You want a shirt cleaned?"

"Naw, you brain-dead little turd. Look at it."

I hold up the T-shirt, gripping it between clenched fingers. It's black. Size small. The price tag is still attached. On the front is this awesome graffiti-style yo-yo outlined in red and yellow.

"Think it'll fit?" Rozelle asks.

I'm speechless.

"You gotta know I'll be makin' a few changes, Low-Cal. Like that shirt you were wearin' the other day." She sticks her finger into her mouth and pretends to gag. "I gotta update your wardrobe." When I don't speak, she says, "What the hell's wrong with you?" She reaches over the counter to tap her fist against my head. "Don't be goin' stupid when you're yo-yoin' or I'll have to get at you." Her fist relaxes. "Well, gotta go now." She jabs a thumb at her posse. "Sasha and Annette are waitin'."

Rozelle pushes open the door with her hip, swings her fleshy arm in a final salute and then she's gone.

I sit with a thump on Gran's swivel chair. What just happened? Did Rozelle bring me a gift, bought with my own money, right after she threatened me?

I thought she'd spend the money on herself. Is she actually trying to help? Yeah, right.

I swivel the chair back and forth, twisting the shirt in my hands. I don't know what Rozelle is up to. I don't know how to get rid of her. I don't know if I can resist wearing the shirt.

I throw the shirt on the counter and pull the chair up to the computer. When I find my favorite yo-yo site, I begin scrolling through the latest models. I'll choose what I want before asking Gran to charge it. No matter how much Rozelle interferes, I won't let her ruin my plans.

The perfume hits me first. Three scents blended into a toxic cloud: Rozelle's is like getting assaulted by flowers; Sasha's is musky; Annette's is apple-scented. All of it is mixed with the sweat and stink from an afternoon in hot classrooms with no air-conditioning. My eyes water. My nose runs.

There's the clunk of Rozelle's boots on the sidewalk. The click of Annette's high heels, as if she needs to be taller. The swish of Sasha's spandex. And the constant chatter from them all, most of it mocking me.

My blood thuds in my ears with each step. They swing their brown limbs, which gleam in the sun. I walk with stiff arms, trying to avoid the electrifying shock I get if they brush against me. I hang my head since my eyes are at the same altitude as certain body parts that bounce when they walk. I can't seem to stop staring.

They hustle me to the parkette exactly seven days after my first busking attempt, just like I promised my crowd.

An old car rattles by on the street. Water splashes in the fountain. Two boys are waiting near the bench where I performed last time. They have eager faces, their cheap plastic yo-yos ready to throw.

"Hey, can you teach us some tricks?"

They're a cool breeze on this stifling day. A flashback to a younger me. I remember feeling impatient to learn new tricks, amazed by what others could do in online videos, desperate to figure out their moves.

"He's busy." Rozelle pushes in front of me before I can answer. Sasha and Annette imprison me on either side.

I frown and slither sideways between them without making contact. The boys look dejected. "Find me after," I say. "I'll show you some moves then."

"Awesome. Thanks!" They scoot away from the girls' glares, flashing enthusiastic grins at me.

"Let's get it goin', Low-Cal." Rozelle nudges my shoulder.

Even though her touch is electric, I don't flinch. "You didn't have to scare them," I say.

"Scare them!" Sasha hoots. "Good idea." She tiptoes after them, her hands extended above her head like claws, a demented look on her face.

Rozelle yanks her back by an exposed bra strap.

"If that scares 'em, they deserve it," Rozelle says, ignoring Sasha's scowl.

Annette giggles. Sasha kicks her where the strap of her high-heeled shoe crosses over her ankle bone.

"Ow!" Annette hops on one foot to rub her ankle.

"Besides, I can't have you givin' private performances to little snots," Rozelle continues. "No money in it." She heads off, trusting we'll follow. "Come on. We'll set up over there."

I step in line behind Rozelle with a sigh. I'm like a dog on a leash, getting tugged wherever my master leads. I hate following her, but I don't know how to get free.

We set up between the street corner and the fountain. The jewelry shop is on the far side of the parkette, beyond the fountain. I don't want a face-off with the jeweler again.

"Where's the shirt?" Rozelle demands.

"Under this one." I lift my old T-shirt to reveal the one she bought with money I earned.

"Then get ready."

"Stop telling me what to do."

Her jaw muscles ripple. "Don't push me, Low-Cal."

If I were a cartoon character, I'd have a black cloud over my head.

I turn away to pull off my old T-shirt. I don't want an audience yet. The yo-yo shirt underneath rides up, exposing my bony ribcage and hairless chest.

My back goes stiff as I anticipate the jabs. *Scrawny. One bite.* I'm making up the jokes for them now. I struggle out of the old shirt as fast as possible and then yank the yo-yo one back down.

On the street, a cyclist races to get ahead of a bus belching out diesel clouds. I smooth the yo-yo design flat on my chest. I can't help but admire it, but I don't want Rozelle to know. No point in giving her more ammunition.

I spin around to catch the end of a glaring session between Sasha and Annette. Rozelle is fetching an old milk crate from the stack in front of Lucky Convenience. The two boys are watching me from near the fountain.

"Not bad." Annette nods at me.

I squirm. Is she mocking me? I drop my old shirt, fish a yo-yo from my pocket. It's the neon one. My twin racers haven't come yet.

"What did I tell you?" Rozelle drops the crate at my feet. "You can dress him up."

"Oooh! Roz's getting hot!" Sasha teases.

Rozelle's glare shuts her down.

"Get on with it, Low-Cal." Rozelle pronounces my name with malice, probably to make it clear that she could never like me.

My hands shake as I position the loop of string around my middle finger. I'm a mess, and it's Rozelle's fault. I slap my hat on the ground in front of the crate. For a brief moment, I consider refusing to perform, although I can already feel the jabs to my gut that would be sure to follow. Anyway, I want to perform. I want to get a rush from the crowd again.

I climb onto the milk crate and begin to warm up. I stretch my arms back to loosen my shoulders, and I throw a few sidestyle. The girls flank me—Sasha on my left, Annette on the right, Rozelle center front. A built-in audience I'd rather do without.

When a sideways loop slices close to Annette's ear, she yelps. "Watch it!"

"Sorry." I fight a smile as they all step back. Then I start into my new lineup of tricks.

Dealing with Rozelle has made me forget how jittery I am, till now. My hands start to sweat, and my heart beats faster. I hope I can pull in a crowd. I hope I don't screw up any tricks.

For this routine, I had to stay up late, practicing in the darkened shop. A few of the tricks still make me nervous, especially the atomic bomb—the one I messed up most often. I'm not sure I can do it under pressure.

I toss a few vertical punches, trying to work my way into the zone.

Calm down. Breathe. You can do this.

I think only of my feet on the milk crate, the string around my finger, my yo-yo flying through the air.

When I can imagine pulling off my first trick flawlessly, I suck in a load of oxygen and begin.

I throw a hard sleeper and pinch the string about a hand's length from the spinning yo-yo. I swing the yo-yo in a small circle a few times and then release the string, tugging the yo-yo back to my hand. A pinwheel. I repeat it three more times, turning on my box after each toss, hoping people from every direction will come to watch my show.

The two boys yell and hurry over, raising heads throughout the parkette. The old men are here again, arguing on benches by the fountain. They glance over and return to their loud talk, obviously not impressed by yo-yo moves.

"That was great!" one boy says. The boys push in front of Rozelle.

I smile down at my audience of two—Rozelle and her girls are only here for money. My money.

My next trick is shaky. I'm letting Rozelle get to me. I block out everything but the yo-yo as I skin-the-cat, an easy trick to get me back on track.

A crowd slowly gathers. When I've got about ten people watching, I make a move. I jump off the milk crate and land with both feet on the ground, liking how it startles Rozelle.

"Hold your arm out sideways," I say to one of the boys, my best—maybe my only—fans. I throw the yo-yo perpendicular to his arm.

He yelps but holds still.

The yo-yo loops around his bare forearm from underneath, circling up and over to land back on the string between us. A trapeze.

"Wow!" The boys' eyes are huge. There's a smattering of applause.

I flip the yo-yo back around and take a quick bow. I'm itching for more, eager to feel in control of the crowd.

Back on my crate, I form a one-handed star out of the yo-yo string and then a two-handed star. More people are gathering. A guy in his twenties wearing a funky fedora eyes me critically. I wonder if he can toss a trick. I want to impress him if I can.

I toss another hard sleeper, making sure the yo-yo is vertical, not leaning to the side. I swing the string behind my yo-yo arm, so that the yo-yo hangs draped over my tricep. I grab the string just above the spinning yo-yo and jerk the yo-yo up and over my arm. A pop-the-clutch.

The crowd claps. I notice the fedora guy nodding. I can't stop grinning. I'm riding high, ready for my next trick.

Just then, the jewelry store owner pushes through to the front, his glasses perched low on his nose, his hair combed over his bald spot. Not him again.

"My store was robbed last week," he yells up at me.

I'm doing a warp drive, trying to concentrate on the trick.

"They came a few hours after you left."

Can't Rozelle act like a manager and get rid of this guy? The man's gesturing too close to my huge loops, which I shift sideways, making the yo-yo quiver.

"But I was ready, see? I knew you were up to something. I called the cops before those punks got to me, and they got nothing but a ride in the police car. All except one." The man's eyes narrow. "He got away."

What's he saying? I move into a brain twister, but I have too much slack on the string and the yo-yo smacks my knuckles hard. It dive bombs. My knuckles sting. I call the yo-yo back to my hand and toss it out again.

"So you were checking out my store last week, weren't you?" The man's still talking. "Admit it. You were the lookout."

"What?" He's accusing me?

People in the crowd mutter. How can I make this guy shut up?

"You have to be involved somehow"—he pokes a finger at me—"because you knew what was about to happen."

"I didn't—"

"Come on, Low-Cal." Rozelle is beside the jeweler now, and for a moment I'm glad to see her. "I saw what you did last week. Tell the poor man the truth."

"No, don't...," I begin, still trying to concentrate on my routine, to save my show. I can tell from the tone of her voice that I'm not going to like what she says.

"Listen, I know this guy," Rozelle says to the jeweler. "He goes to my school. And I've seen him do this before." She nods dramatically.

"Don't listen to her!" I say. I don't know what she's up to, but I know it'll end with me getting hurt.

"Don't be so modest, Low-Cal." Rozelle sounds innocent, even kind. How does she play the part so well? "He doesn't like to brag, but...he's got a knack for seein' things—before they happen."

"What?" I'm almost at the atomic-bomb trick, but it's Rozelle that I want to blow up.

A murmur runs through the crowd. A few people laugh.

"Yeah, his mind goes somewhere when he yo-yos. Then he says things that usually come true."

"That's ridiculous." The man snorts. "He's a thief, not a prophet."

"A prophet! That's it!" Rozelle's tone brightens like she's been given a gift. "He said last week that you were tough enough to get rid of any thieves. You're so busy accusin' him that you're not seein' how he predicted what would happen." She zeroes in on the two eager boys still clutching their yo-yos. "You were here last week. Remember?"

I'm still trying to keep my yo-yo moving, but I manage to see the boys nodding enthusiastically.

"That's not how it—," I begin.

"If you don't believe me, see for yourself." Rozelle grabs my hat. "Who wants to hear from the Yo-Yo Prophet?" She waves the hat, ready for donations.

A hush falls over the crowd, and I'm relieved. No one will fall for it.

"I do!" says an overweight woman. Her face is blotchy, bloated, sad. "Ask him if I'll find a job soon." She drops a five-dollar bill in the hat.

I hate where this is going. "I can't—"

"Come on," Rozelle pretends to plead. "These people need you."

I shake my head, start my atomic-bomb trick instead. I flip the yo-yo over my left hand and under my right before I mount the spinning yo-yo on the string. I can't think about the woman, the jeweler, Rozelle, the crowd. I can only think about the string around my fingers, the yo-yo's position, the warmth building in my chest, my steady breathing.

Sasha and Annette start a chant. "Yo-Yo! Pro-phet! Yo-Yo! Pro-phet!" A few others join in. So many faces, watching, waiting, for me.

Still working the atomic bomb, I shoot the yo-yo back and forth from one string segment to another, my thoughts tossing like the yo-yo.

"Please," the woman pleads. "I've been out of work so long…"

Answer her, Rozelle's glare says.

"I…uh…" Is it so wrong to give this woman hope? She's obviously upset. What's the worst than can happen? "Sure you will. Next week," I hear myself say.

My stomach thunks as soon as the words leave me. I'm no better than Rozelle—lying to these people.

The crowd hums with whispers and muttering. The woman clasps her hands together. I'm spinning the atomic bomb now. The trick is working, but my hands are shaking. Sweat is beading on my forehead. My head feels like it's going to explode.

"If he's a prophet, then I'm a monkey," the jewelry store owner says.

The hum from the crowd gets louder. I try to forget about my lie by finishing the atomic-bomb trick with a spectacular Ferris-wheel dismount. The crowd breaks into a fit of cheering. The air crackles with energy.

I'm liking the attention, the heat from the crowd. Still, the prediction nags at me. I wonder what I've gotten into. How is that woman going to feel when she realizes I'm a fraud?

I end my show with a repeat of my atomic bomb. My moves are radioactive now. Red hot. The crowd hoots and claps. The jeweler marches back to his store.

After the show, I teach the two boys the dizzy baby, which they love. People compliment me while Sasha and Annette collect the cash and Rozelle chats up the jobless woman. When the crowd thins, Rozelle grabs the cash—more bills than last time—and stuffs about half into my backpack. I'm about to insist on more when she thumps me on the shoulder, sending another electric pulse that knocks me off-guard. "Good job, Yo-Yo Prophet."

She didn't call me Low-Cal. I don't know if Sasha and Annette notice, but I do. It shouldn't matter, but it does.

"Uh...thanks." I feel like I've shed my old too-small skin. Grown larger. Sleeker.

Rozelle ignores me.

I let her keep the cash.

6

The next Saturday morning, Gran is browning sausages and cooking scrambled eggs in the same pan, her white hair like a hovering cloud. I'm setting the table, disgusted by the fried tomatoes already shriveled and steaming on the plates. I hate fried tomatoes, but Gran loves them, so I don't say anything.

"Calvin, how did your street performance go with your little"—her eyes scan the room as if she's searching for the missing word—"your little toy?"

My jaw tightens. "Gran, it's not a toy."

"Sorry, dear. You're right." She scoops up some egg with a spatula and then slops it onto the counter, missing the plates entirely.

My stomach knots. "Let me help."

"I've got it." Her lips press together. She smears bits of egg around on the counter before she rescues most of it. She stabs the sausages one by one, dropping them to land on the plates beside the egg.

I add the thick slices of buttered toast and carry the plates, one in each hand, unable to avoid the stench of greasy tomatoes.

Our table-for-two is shoved between the fridge and the end of the counter. I squeeze into my chair, leaving room on Gran's side for her to sit easily.

"Nothing like a proper British breakfast," she says as she always does, crumpling into her chair with a sigh.

"Just like your mother used to make," I reply. It's our little Saturday-morning routine. I sit, remembering how my mother used to serve noodle soup for breakfast.

A cough begins deep in Gran's chest, rumbling up to explode from her mouth.

I leap up. "You okay, Gran?"

Her head is turned away from the food. One sleeve of her bathrobe dips into her tea. She gulps, blinks back tears and nods. Then she wipes her sleeve and turns back to her plate, squishing a tomato in half with her fork. "The yo-yo," she says, finally remembering the word. "How did it go with the yo-yo?"

I sit again, heart racing. What's wrong with her? Watching my mom get sick was bad enough. I can't take it if Gran gets sick too.

The tomatoes are fleshy, wrinkled. I push mine off to the side and grab a piece of toast. "It was pretty good." I crunch my toast loudly, wondering how I could ever explain about the Yo-Yo Prophet.

"Pretty good? What does that mean?" Gran cuts into a sausage.

"I performed twice, over at Mason Parkette." Just thinking about that blur of faces, and the applause, makes me smile. "It was incredible, Gran. They loved me."

"That's not incredible. Of course they did."

I shovel in some eggs and talk with my mouth full. "I did most of my tricks okay, even the atomic bomb. The people were awesome. I felt like I could make them cheer whenever I wanted."

Gran chuckles, bringing on a small fit of coughing. "Sounds like fun."

"It was great." I drop my fork, remembering. "They were yelling and clapping for more...and then they started calling me—" I stop abruptly, pick up my fork and shovel in another mouthful.

"What did they call you?"

I shrug. “Nothing,” I say with my mouth full. I can’t tell Gran about the Yo-Yo Prophet, or how I let Rozelle take over my show and make me lie. “After, there were these two kids who wanted to learn some tricks. And this girl from school gave me a yo-yo T-shirt to wear.”

“I’m glad you’re making friends.”

Yeah, right. Friends. I’m not an idiot. I’m just Rozelle’s fool, her cash grab. I grip my fork tighter. I can’t let Rozelle push me around.

Gran forks her second tomato. The insides squirt out like blood from a wound.

I wince. “Gran, I have to tell you something.” I push my plate away.

“What is it, Calvin?”

“I don’t like fried tomatoes.” I hold my breath.

“You don’t?” Gran’s face falls. Her brows bunch together.

I take a breath. “Yeah. I really hate them. I always have.”

“Why didn’t you tell me? All these years, I could have had your share.” She grins and leans over to spear one of my tomatoes.

I grin back. That was easy. Now it gets harder. “And there’s something else.”

“You don’t like sausages either?” Gran eyes my plate.

"No, they're okay. It's Spader. How do you know we can trust him?"

Gran sighs. "Mr. Spider? Why shouldn't we trust him?"

"His name's Spader. And I just want to be sure he's offering you a fair deal. Because you don't have to sell the shop, if the deal isn't good. I could help out more. So could Van, if we ask her."

"Mr. Spider is fine. So is the deal." Gran presses her lips together again. "I've thought this through, and checked the paperwork thoroughly."

"Okay." I pause. "So where will we move to?"

"I'll find us a place. Maybe a small house with a garden. I've always wanted a garden."

"Do we have enough time to find a place? It's June fourth already. We need to move by August first."

"It'll be fine." Gran wipes her mouth with her napkin and then crumples it in her fist. "I know you're nervous about the changes. This isn't easy for me either." Her blue eyes hold my gaze. "Selling the shop is like giving up a piece of your grandfather. We started it together, you know, over forty years ago. And with him gone, and Richard, and your mother, well..." Her voice falters. "It's hard to leave it behind."

"I know," I say, only I'm afraid that Gran's slowly leaving me behind as well.

"I just can't keep up anymore." She leans her elbows on the table and rests her head in her hands. "And there's nothing you or I can do about that." Her voice is muffled.

When she looks up again, her face is drained of color and the fine hairs on her upper lip stand out darker than usual.

"Okay, Gran," I say, even though nothing is okay. Not the defeated look on her face. Not the helpless way I feel.

"It's the right thing to do, Calvin."

I stare down at my half-eaten breakfast. I hope she's right.

•••

Three days later, I'm leaving the school cafeteria when Sasha stops me.

"Roz wants to see you," she says.

"But I have to get to class."

"So?"

I check my watch. Seventeen minutes till math with Mr. Marnello. Enough time to tell Rozelle that I'm in charge of my show, not her. "Okay."

Sasha rolls her eyes, one hand on her hip. "I love how you think you have a choice."

She strides down the hall like a model on a runway and heads out the nearest doors. I trail her, wondering where we're going.

We end up at the burger joint across the street—it's where the cool people hang out. I cross into Rozelle's turf, tight-fisted and wary.

The fluorescent lights are too bright. The smell of grease reminds me of Gran's fried tomatoes. There's a long counter for ordering and a few tables bolted to the floor in the back. Rozelle is lounging on one table, swinging her legs and barking orders at Annette, who sits on a chair at the next table.

"Hold my drink, would ya? And gimme a couple of fries."

Annette leaps to do her bidding. Roz leans back on one arm—she's the queen of burgers and fries.

"What are you ordering?" the guy behind the counter asks me.

Sasha strolls on by.

"If you come in here, you buy something!" He's got a moustache as wide as a strip of bacon and a twitch in one eye that makes me freeze solid.

"Be good, Yo-Yo," Rozelle drawls. "Angelo throws dishes when he gets cranky."

Angelo grins. He picks up an empty stainless-steel bowl and tosses it playfully from one hand to another.

I pull out enough change to buy the cheapest thing on the menu—a small orange soda. I don't argue, mostly because I don't want to be late for Mr. Marnello's class. Math is hard enough without pissing him off.

While I'm waiting for my drink, I notice that a few other people have dared to enter Rozelle's palace. A long-haired guy with a mean stare makes me nervous, and a skinny guy from our school gives me the once-over before turning away.

Angelo bangs my cup on the counter, sloshing soda over the edge.

I jump. "Uh, thanks. Do you...uh...have a straw?"

He rolls his eyes. "You want me to drink it for you too?"

Rozelle and her girls laugh. My back goes rigid. My face heats up.

Angelo motions behind me. "Straws are with the lids, kid." He gets out a damp cloth and vigorously wipes the counter.

I get my straw and lid, hands jittery. I head to the back, where Sasha's up on the table beside Rozelle, looking down on Annette with a smirk. When Rozelle sees me coming, she pushes Sasha off and pats the empty space beside her.

"Sit here," she orders.

I obey without thinking. Sasha stomps over to sit beside Annette, who gives her a look that says, *Now you know what it's like*. Sasha glares at me, making me squirm. I sip my soda without tasting it. The skinny guy is watching, probably wondering what Queen Rozelle is doing with a nobody like me.

Rozelle puts an arm around my shoulders, and I stiffen.

"Welcome to my office," she says.

Annette lets out a high-pitched giggle. She's got her legs crossed, swinging one foot and eating fries while enjoying Rozelle's show. Rozelle is watching me as she talks, her face too close to mine, her breath smelling of fries. I stare straight ahead, gripping my soda.

"So here's how I wanna run it," Rozelle begins. "You start the act with yo-yo tricks, and then you use the prophet angle for the finale. I'm gonna ask the crowd who wants a prediction—it's better if I find the best situation for you to predict."

"But—," I begin.

"Only one prediction for each performance. I don't wanna tire you out." She winks at her girls, and I wonder why. "Don't get too specific either. Keep it loose, easy to interpret."

"Roz, I was thinking…," Sasha says.

"You don't wanna be doin' that," Rozelle replies.

Annette guffaws.

Sasha's face goes red, but she keeps talking. "Maybe we could check out a few fortune-tellers, see how they make predictions."

"Naw." Rozelle waves away Sasha's idea. "The Yo-Yo Prophet knows how to handle it."

Now Sasha's really glowering. Rozelle gives my shoulder a squeeze, and I almost drop my drink. I'm wearing shorts and she's in a miniskirt, so our bare legs are touching. It's awkward, electrifying, disturbing. I try to wriggle free, but Rozelle's grip is too tight.

"I don't know." I choke out the words. "I've had enough of that prophet stuff. I just want to do my yo-yo tricks."

"No way." Rozelle shakes her head. "Think 'bout it. Yo-yo tricks are good, but you need more if you wanna stand out. The Yo-Yo Prophet is a better act. It gives 'em entertainment and inspiration."

I grit my teeth. Tell her you're in charge, I think. But I can't make myself say the words.

"Remember, you still owe me—," Rozelle begins.

"Owe you! Because you didn't beat me up when I accidentally bumped into you?" I'm about to explode, but I force myself to be calm. "I think we should call it even. I can take care of things myself."

"Yeah? Like you took care of that frickin' jewelry store guy?" Rozelle snorts. "You need me as much as I need you, Yo-Yo Prophet. And I ain't walkin' away."

"But I'm no prophet," I say. "That was just some stupid...I mean...wild scheme you thought up to make more money. Well, I don't care about the money. And I don't like lying."

"Not a prophet, huh?" Rozelle stares me down.

"That's right." My soda's starting to sweat in the heat. Drops of condensation trickle down the cup and onto my hand.

"Well, you may wanna know that a certain unemployed woman found work today." Rozelle gazes intently at me. "Eleanor Rizzo—the woman from your show at the park—just called." She slides off the table and worms a cell phone from her skirt pocket.

"Yeah?" I leap to my feet, relieved to put some distance between us.

Rozelle waves her cell phone. "Some copy shop downtown needed help."

"Good for her. Although I'm sure I had nothing to do with it." I drop my drink on a table and turn to leave. "Forget this. I've got to get to math."

Behind the counter, Angelo slams the fridge shut and bangs a few plates around.

"Just a minute," Rozelle says. "I've got somethin' you wanna hear."

"I don't want to—"

"Just shut up and listen." She starts pressing buttons on her phone. The skinny guy from our school gets up to leave.

I guess he's trying to get to class on time. Rozelle holds her phone in front of my face. A woman's voice comes through the speaker. She sounds happy.

"Hi Rozelle. This is Eleanor. I just had to tell you that I got the job at Kopy Kingdom. It's the night shift, which isn't great, but I start tomorrow! Please, tell the Yo-Yo Prophet how grateful I am. Without him, I couldn't have done it, mostly because I didn't believe I could. He changed my life. And so did you, Rozelle. Thanks for the—"

Rozelle snaps the phone shut, stopping the message. "The rest is personal," she says.

I can't believe Rozelle would want to get personal with that woman. "Did you get her that job?"

"Naw. It was all you. You predicted it. Then it happened. That's all that matters." Rozelle's eyes are wide. Her voice is smooth, easy.

"So why were you talking to her after my show?"

"I was just checkin' out the crowd." Rozelle slides her phone back into her pocket. "And I was gettin' her number so we could find out when she got a job."

Yeah, right. "Why would you care?"

"Advertisin', stupid. Your prediction came true. She loves you for it. And she's willin' to tell her story to whoever will listen."

I refuse to tell Rozelle that she sounds more like a manager all the time. "But I don't want her to tell anyone about it."

"Why not? If it brings the crowds, who cares what she says?"

"But I don't want to predict—"

"Think 'bout it." Rozelle drapes her arm around my shoulder again, making me tense. "You're just givin' 'em what they want." She pauses. "Hope."

"But..." Hope? That kind of makes sense.

Rozelle squeezes me closer. Her arm is hot, heavy. "And the Yo-Yo Prophet is a cool name."

I pull away. "I know."

"And the money is sweet. Don't tell me you can't use the money."

I think of all the cool yo-yos I could buy. "Sure I can."

"Damn right. So what's the problem? You're not givin' up on me, are you?"

"No. I mean, yes. I mean, this is my show, not yours. I should decide what happens."

There. I said it. I brace for Rozelle's anger. She'll hit me, or at least threaten me. But she doesn't do either.

"Oh, I get it," Rozelle says. "This is 'bout creative control." Her eyebrows knot. "You run the show. I take care of the rest. I've heard 'bout this—with musicians and stuff."

I'm so relieved that I'm not getting hit. "Well, I—"

"I can work with that," Rozelle says. "So you plan your tricks, decide when to do the prediction. We'll scope out the next venue." She nods at Sasha and Annette. "I figure we should move it up. Find a boss location."

"That...sounds good." Have I just made another deal with Rozelle? I check my watch. Two minutes till class. I'll never make it.

"How's Saturday? We could meet here in the mornin'. Maybe at nine?"

"I...guess so." I glance over the long counter and out the grimy front windows. No one's hanging around on the school grounds. Even the smokers on the sidewalk have gone in.

"Then it's settled." She grins. "Now get out of here." She pushes me toward the exit. "Don't be late for class."

"Yeah, and get the homework for us," Sasha says.

Annette laughs and then stuffs a fry in her mouth.

I spin away from them, feeling light-headed. I'm not sure who's pulling the strings now, but I hope it's me. I push the door open, squinting at the sunlight. I'll get detention, for sure. And I'll probably show up on Saturday, just for kicks.

I can practice yo-yo tricks night and day before a show. I can do study group with Mr. Marnello before the fractions test. But some things I will never be ready for.

I spent four days perfecting new yo-yo tricks and debating whether I should meet up with Rozelle. Now, it's Saturday morning, and I'm standing in the men's washroom at Angelo's burger place, face to chest with Rozelle. I can't breathe. I can't look straight ahead.

"The yo-yo shirt's a start, but you need to pimp up." Rozelle reaches out, smears my hair with fruity-smelling gel and then rubs it in a little too thoroughly.

"I like my hair the way it is." I edge sideways. The air is stifling, and the urinals stink. I hope no one else comes in. I couldn't take it.

She yanks me back. "Come on, Yo-Yo. We made a deal. You can run the show, but I gotta do somethin' 'bout your look." She frowns. "And it ain't easy."

I glare, keeping my chin tilted up, away from the view of what's busting out of her lace-trimmed tank top.

She wrenches tufts of my hair upright. Her arm muscles ripple with each pull. Her bracelets clang together. The tugging lasts a painfully long time. Squirming just makes her clasp a gooey hand onto my scrawny bicep.

I try to jerk free. "Let go." Does she know how hard she squeezes?

"Then stay still." She releases me.

More tugging. She takes a step back, tilts her head sideways, squints and studies my head.

"I guess that'll do." She slides to one side, leaving me in front of the mirror. "What do you think?"

The fluorescent lights make me look disturbingly pale with big hollows under my eyes. As for my hair—I guess it's okay. It's spiked and wet-looking, as if I'd just toweled it dry.

Rozelle's head appears above mine. "Better than mattin' it down anyway."

"It looks like I just got out of the shower."

She shakes her head, making her dangly earrings swing. "You got no taste." She tries to rearrange a few strands, but I jerk away. She scowls. "Did you at least watch how I did it?"

"How could I see? You were standing in front of me!"

"This is serious, Yo-Yo. Your dweeb image has to go." She grabs my hand and slaps the tube of gel into it. "Here. Keep it."

"Thanks." I make sure she hears the sarcasm in my voice.

A black cloud passes over Rozelle's face. She goes to grab my shirt—the yo-yo one she gave me—and then stops. She rearranges her face into a forced smile. "I better see you usin' it. My gifts don't go to waste."

"Sure." I hold back a grin. Making her angry is kind of satisfying now that I know she won't hit me. I mean, why would she damage her meal ticket?

I shove the gel into my bag as we exit the men's washroom together, which is too weird. Sasha and Annette are leaning against the counter, looking lean, brown and tough. Angelo's forcing a guy I recognize from school to buy a coffee.

"Nice hair." Annette raises her eyebrows at me. She's wearing a skimpy dress with heels, while Sasha's in tight jean shorts and a sparkly top. I can't stop my eyes from skating over them.

"What were you two doing in there?" Sasha sneers. "Did you need a little alone time?"

"Shut up," Rozelle and I say at the same time. We glance at each other, surprised.

Sasha hoots. "They're even starting to sound the same." She nudges Annette, who hides her smile with one hand.

"Now, play nice while we have company, kids." Rozelle flips her straightened hair in Sasha's face as she turns to smile at the guy buying coffee.

Sasha glares at me like I'm to blame for my own existence.

"This is Marshall," Rozelle says. "And this"—she shoves me forward—"is the Yo-Yo Prophet."

"Uh…hi." I shuffle from foot to foot, wondering why he's here. He must be in grade eleven or twelve. Too old to want to talk to me.

Marshall sips his coffee, examining me through the steam. He's got a hard set to his mouth and a skeptical expression on his narrow face. His hair is almost shoulder length—blond with wide chunks of orange and pink. The nose piercing is okay, but the bar through his lip disturbs me.

"Is it true that yo-yos were once used as weapons?" Marshall asks me.

Strange first question. "Weapons?" I say. I see Rozelle and the girls perk up. Not surprising.

"Yeah, I read that sixteenth-century hunters in the Philippines would tie a rock to a long cord and throw it at their prey." Marshall steps closer as he talks. He's taller than Rozelle but not by much. "Apparently the hunters could pull the rock back like a yo-yo."

Sasha pretends to throw a rock at me. I ignore her.

"Maybe they did," I say. "But it's not the same as a yo-yo."

"What do you mean?"

"When a yo-yo hits something, it loses spin and can't return."

"Of course." Marshall sets his coffee on the counter and pulls out a notebook and pen from his back pocket. Behind the counter, Angelo flips a burger, which sizzles and spits on the grill.

"Marshall blogs 'bout cool stuff, Yo-Yo. Lotsa people at school follow him," Rozelle says. "He's gonna blog 'bout you. Maybe post a few photos or a video. Spread the word online."

"He is?" My chest gets tight.

"Yup." Marshall tucks a strand of orange hair behind his ear. "If there's a good story." He flips to a blank page and starts writing.

I swallow hard. No pressure.

"Okay, let's get goin'. You can talk on the way," Rozelle says.

"Where are we going?" I ask warily.

"You'll see when we get there."

"But I—"

"Just worry 'bout your tricks, Yo-Yo. I'll do the rest. Remember?" Rozelle points to a huge portable stereo on one of the tables. "Sasha and Annette, you'll be carryin' that."

"What's that for?" I'm getting more jittery by the moment.

"I'm makin' improvements," Rozelle says. "You got the shirt and the new do, now we need tunes for our show."

Annette grabs the handle and yanks, barely lifting the stereo off the table before she drops it. "Ugh. It weighs a ton!"

"I don't need music...," I begin.

"It's a relic." Sasha rolls her eyes. "Where'd you get it? King Tut's tomb?"

"It's my brother's." Rozelle glares. "And I carried it here, no problem."

"Roz, it's too heavy," Annette whines.

"Yeah, *we're* both skinny," Sasha adds, and I know she's implying that Rozelle isn't.

"This'll help you bulk up." Rozelle hurls the words at Sasha, her jaw muscles clenching and unclenching.

Then she links arms with me like she owns me. "You gotta earn your way, just like Yo-Yo and me."

My arm is burning where it touches hers, but I wait till we head out to pull free. Rozelle waves goodbye to Angelo, whose eye is still twitching like crazy. Now that I know him a bit, it doesn't bother me as much. Marshall leaves his coffee behind; he's still scribbling notes.

As we walk the one block to the subway, Sasha and Annette lag behind, struggling with the stereo. When Marshall hangs back to ask them a question, I whisper to Rozelle. "Are you sure this is a good idea? The blog, I mean?"

"'Course it is. We gotta get the word out 'bout you."

"But no one at school knows that I do yo-yo tricks. Except you. And them." I stab a finger toward Sasha and Annette.

"Soon they'll all know, Yo-Yo."

"That's what I'm afraid of."

"You worry too much." She elbows me in the ribs.

I wince. Then I notice Marshall has caught up to us, and he's listening to every word.

I shut up. It's bad enough that he's blogging about my yo-yoing. He doesn't need to blog about my fears too.

On the subway, Marshall sits on the bench opposite me. Rozelle sits beside me, and Sasha and Annette are one seat over. As the subway rocks, Rozelle knocks against me, but I can't move away since I'm already jammed against the edge of the seat. Marshall asks questions nonstop. What tricks can I do? How did I start yo-yoing? I try to answer well, even though my heart is racing and my face feels hot. Marshall writes everything down.

He asks, "What type of yo-yos do you use?"

Rozelle hovers over my shoulder like she's afraid I'm going to make a mistake.

"Uh, any kind. I've got about eight different ones so far."

"Do you use them all in your show?"

"No, just this one." I pull my favorite neon yo-yo out of my backpack. "It's a...uh...modified yo-yo—good for string and looping tricks."

Marshall glances up from his scribbling. He nods.

"And I just got two new yo-yos in the mail. I've been... uh...trying some two-handed tricks." Should I have said that?

"Two-handed tricks?" Rozelle interrupts. "Why didn't I hear 'bout this?"

"I didn't know it mattered to you." I sink lower in my seat.

"Everythin' you do matters to me, Yo-Yo."

I frown.

"Will you be using those today?" Marshall asks.

"Not yet. I've got to practice with them a bit more." A lot more.

"You should go for it today," Rozelle says. "Take it up a notch."

"No." I fiddle with my yo-yo, wishing I could break into a few tricks. "I didn't even bring them."

Rozelle crosses her arms, muscles tight. "Next time."

"If I'm ready."

"How often do you practice?" Marshall's still writing.

"All the time." I don't tell him it's what I do to relax. It sounds like I have no life.

"And what about those predictions?" Marshall flips back through his notebook, scans a page. "You predicted a robbery and...a job offer?"

It sounds lame when he says it. "I guess." I shrug.

Rozelle leans in. "The predictions came true."

"But I don't know if it'll happen again," I add. In fact, I'm pretty sure I'll never do it again, no matter what Rozelle wants.

"It will." Rozelle tosses me a frustrated look. "It happens when he doesn't expect it. He'll be doin' his hardest tricks and then...*boom*...he comes out with this random comment 'bout someone in the crowd. It's pretty cool."

"Uh-huh." Marshall sounds unconvinced.

"It's not that cool," I say.

I stare at Marshall's tiny, neat writing, but I can't read what it says upside down. What if his blog post makes me look stupid?

We get off at Union Station and walk east. Everything feels wrong. My hands are sweating. My hair feels stiff. How am I supposed to perform with stiff hair?

"Tell me where we're going," I say to Rozelle when we reach the St. Lawrence Market. I can't stand not knowing.

"Right there." Rozelle points to an open area on the north side of the street, where the market has spilled outside.

We weave between the cars that are stopped for the light. Across the street, a few small trees shade the vendors selling fruits and vegetables at makeshift tables. Baskets overflow with strawberries, herbs and tomatoes, scenting the air and making me feel queasy. Throngs of people mill among the tables, squeezing fruit, browsing, haggling. They don't look ready for a show.

Sasha and Annette drop the stereo near a low brick wall that arcs around a concrete-lined pond. Annette moans. Sasha rubs her shoulder. Marshall sits on the brick wall, his pen perched behind his ear and a camera in one hand. His eyes never leave me.

"This place is hoppin'." Rozelle glances at the Saturday crowd.

"Are we allowed to perform here?" I cringe. Too many people. Why would they want to watch me?

"Sure we are, Yo-Yo. You just get ready."

As we set up, Eleanor Rizzo—the woman I predicted would get a job—appears. I glare at Rozelle, who must have invited her, but she's busy introducing Eleanor to Marshall, who starts interviewing her. No one asks me if this is what I want.

I pull out my yo-yo and toss a few. Eleanor looks different—brighter, happier, better dressed. As she answers Marshall's questions about my last show, it bugs me that I can't get a clear idea of what he's thinking, what he might blog about me. His mouth is always set in that same thin line, and his eyes narrow like he doesn't believe a word he hears.

My scalp feels tight. I'm on edge. When Marshall insists on taking a few photos of Eleanor and me together, I feel guilty, like I'm still lying to her. But I can't let anything get to me. Sasha and Annette are cuing the music—another distraction to deal with.

I step onto the brick wall, which is just wide enough to hold me. Rozelle places a red plastic bucket in front of me. On it, she's painted *Yo-Yo Prophet* in yellow letters. "For all the money we're gonna make," she says. "Get started. Then I'll introduce you."

"Okay." I spin my neon yo-yo in an inside loop, hoping my hands will stay steady.

Rozelle nods to Annette, who's positioned beside the stereo. Marshall starts video-recording my performance, which I try to ignore. The music blares. Heads turn. I throw ten reach-for-the-moons to keep their attention.

"You call this music?" I hear Sasha yell.

A circle of people begins to form around me. I glimpse anger flaring on Rozelle's face, but she stays concentrated on me and the crowd.

"It's Teknonaut," Annette scolds. "Remember? Her brother's techno sound." She nods toward Rozelle.

I'm curious about her brother's music, but I have no time to think. I walk-the-dog along the brick wall.

"Some music!" Sasha hoots. "I predict great success. Does that make me a prophet too?"

I have to agree with Sasha. The music is bizarre: random noises, droning vocals and a techno beat. But I like the steady rhythm. It calms me and lets me focus.

I begin a roller-coaster trick by throwing a trapeze, making the yo-yo loop around the finger of my left hand and then land back on the string. Keeping time with the music, I bounce the yo-yo off the string and swing it to loop around my right hand into another trapeze. Then I send it back again for a double or nothing on the left hand and swing into a dismount.

A few people clap. I soak it up. It's like rain after a drought.

"Isn't he wonderful!" exclaims Eleanor.

I head into my next trick, eager to please.

"Yo, people!" Rozelle yells over the music. "This here's the Yo-Yo Pro-phet!" She sounds like a hip-hop carnival caller. "A pro with a yo-yo! With a knack for predictin' the future!"

Will she ever shut up about that? I move into a zipper—a smooth trick with loads of cool flips.

"Whoa! Look at him go!" I hear a man say.

Everyone's energy is feeding into mine as more people gather. Marshall's staying near the front, his pen still lodged behind his ear, his camera glued to my every move. Annette's chomping on her gum like a cow chewing its cud.

The zipper's a big hit with everyone but Sasha, who's not even watching. I throw a few around-the-worlds. My blood's pulsing, the music's pounding.

Then I sense a disturbance, like I've lost people's attention. I scan between throws. A cop in uniform is striding toward me, his hat pulled low over dark sunglasses.

My legs begin to shake. I switch to a series of loop-the-loops so I can catch what's going on. People turn and gape as the cop pushes through.

He stops between Rozelle and Marshall, right in front of me. Annette's wide-eyed, one hand on the stereo, lowering the music to half volume. Sasha's smirking. The cop tucks one thumb into a utility belt that Batman would be proud of.

"Can I see your permit?" His voice is so deep it rumbles.

"Permit?" I squeak. My yo-yo wobbles in its loop.

A few people laugh, Sasha loudest of all.

Be strong, I tell myself. Keep control.

"You do have one, don't you?" He adjusts his hat. "The City requires it for all street performers."

"Uh..." I glance at Rozelle.

"Officer," Rozelle says, and I recognize that smooth voice she uses on teachers. "I'm his manager. Maybe we could talk over here?" She puts a hand on his arm, tries to lead him away.

The cop's black boots remain planted. "Just show me the permit."

"You don't understand. I'm—"

"Young lady, I'm here to enforce the law, not chat. Now, do you have a permit?"

The crowd murmurs. Rozelle looks tiny next to this cop. I'm just trying to keep the show going—whirling, twisting, endless loops.

"We'll get one tomorrow—," she begins.

"No permit. No performance." He motions to Annette to cut the music, which she does.

My blood still keeps the beat. I've never done so many loops in a row.

"No!" Rozelle yells at Annette, who doesn't move to turn it back on. "Really, sir, we'll only be a few more minutes. Let us finish."

The cop places both hands on his hips. "If you're going to cause a disturbance, miss, I'll have to take you in."

Rozelle blinks. She scoops up the bucket. "Do we still need a permit if we're not collectin' money?"

"That's enough." The cop pulls out a pad of paper and a pen. "What's your name, young lady?"

Rozelle's mouth falls open and then shuts.

No way. Is he going to arrest her? For some reason, this gets to me. Why should she matter?

I rev up. My hands are on fire. My cheeks feel blistered. The yo-yo and I are like a piston engine, gaining power with each crazy revolution.

“Officer, give us another chance, please.” I find my voice, try to sound calm. “It’s not like we’re bothering anyone. We’re not wrecking things or robbing people.” I think of the jewelry store owner. “I mean, there are probably people who need you more than we do.” I try to laugh—make it a joke. “Like, maybe there’s a crime happening around the corner right now?”

Before the cop can react, a police car races down the street, sirens blaring, red-and-blue lights flashing. A few people gasp. Eleanor shrieks. The cop’s head spins so fast it’s unnatural. The radio on his belt crackles to life. The car pulls to a screeching halt a few buildings away. The cop takes off, one hand pulling his radio free.

“Get that permit,” he calls as his boots pound the sidewalk.

People are talking all around me.

“How did he know?”

“I can’t believe it!”

My head is reeling. My yo-yo hangs limp. I can’t remember what trick I was throwing.

“The Yo-Yo Prophet!” Rozelle steps onto the brick wall beside me, her face flushed and gleaming. “You heard it from his own mouth.” She slaps me hard on the back. “This guy can predict the future.” She gives me a sideways look. “He really can.”

Someone begins to clap. Others join in until it fills my ears, flooding me with happiness. Marshall cheers as loud as the rest. Coins ring into the bucket.

They believe her. And for the first time, I do too.

I wake the next day with my hair flattened against my head, the spikes gone, like yesterday never happened.

I should feel deflated—back to my usual boring self—except for the bills and coins on my dresser.

I pick up the stack of bills and fan myself; I run the coins through my fingers, liking the metallic smell. It's more money than I've ever made before. More people swarmed me after the show. And that cop car appearing right after I…

My skin tingles. I still can't believe it. Did I really predict it? Or was it dumb luck?

I flop back onto the tangle of sheets and stare at the peeling paint on the ceiling. I had said what was on my mind. It was instinct. But somehow, it came true. Like in a comic book, when the scrawny guy discovers his special power—sonic speed or immortality—and he's suddenly more than a pathetic loser. He has potential.

Do I have potential?

Is that why Rozelle won't leave me alone?

I sit up with a jerk, craning my neck so I can see into the mirror above my dresser. When I turn to the side, I try to catch a glimpse of my profile. Does my hair really look matted? Not that I care what she thinks.

I pull on a T-shirt and shorts. Rozelle's tube of gel sits on the dresser beside the coins. I snatch it up and squeeze a blob onto my palm. It won't hurt to try. I yank and tug my hair into tufts, like Rozelle did.

It just looks messy.

Who am I kidding?

I rake my hands over my head, trying to scrub off the gel. When I stop, it actually looks not bad. At least, not bad for me. Almost as if Rozelle did it.

I stare at myself in the mirror, wondering if Marshall will write about me—the Yo-Yo Prophet. Maybe he already has. My stomach does a loop-the-loop. I hope he doesn't trash me.

My eyes drift again to the pile of bills and coins—money people threw after I made that prediction—and I get to thinking: If I can predict when Eleanor Rizzo will get a job, or when a crime will happen, can I predict my own future?

I know what I want to happen. I want to be a yo-yo master. To be accepted, even liked. But I also want Gran to get better. And I want this deal with Spader to work out well for us.

So what does my gut tell me will happen?

Only one way to find out. I grab my new red twin racers from my desk and slide the slip-loop onto the middle finger of each hand. There's not much floor space in my room so I scoot into the living room. Gran's nowhere in sight. It's Sunday morning, so maybe she's at the flea market. She hasn't been well enough to go in ages.

Alone with the painted royal faces, I break into alternating two-handed loops. I keep my loops horizontal so I'm throwing above Gran's collection. When I almost hit the Queen Elizabeth II commemorative tankard, I shift backward. I can picture a red yo-yo slicing through the air to explode it. Not good.

My left hand is weaker than my right, although hours of practice have helped. But it isn't just about practice. It's knowing how to feel the yo-yo—when to tug, when to let it out, when it's going off track.

I time my throws so one yo-yo is going out as the other one is coming back. I lose myself in the rhythm of it, my hands shaping the loops. I relax, let mistakes happen, move into the flow of the yo-yos, the endless cycle. They pull away, recover, spin back. I follow the momentum, let it carry me into the zone.

I'm loose yet focused, like riding a bicycle without holding the handlebars.

"What's going to happen to me?" I ask, trying to keep it casual.

I wait one, two, three beats. Then the answers hit like a slap from Rozelle.

I'm practically a yo-yo genius. One yo-yo smacks against my palm. Spader's deal is too good to be true. The other yo-yo thuds home. And Gran's getting sicker.

I slump onto Gran's rose-colored couch, still reeling from my predictions, trying to ignore those stiff china faces with their penetrating eyes. Maybe I can predict the future. Too bad I can't do anything to change it.

I head downstairs to check if Marshall has posted anything; I might as well find out how bad it is. I enter through the back door. The machines are quiet, since it's Sunday, and the chemical smell is faint. I find Gran with Van, clearing out the shelves under the front counter, getting ready for Spader's takeover next week.

Van is on her knees, her blue cotton skirt tucked under her legs. Her head is under the counter, and she's scrubbing the inside of a cupboard with a soapy cloth, her arm muscles like ropes.

Gran is seated on a low stool, gazing into a cardboard box as if she's forgotten what she was doing. Her T-shirt is twisted around her waist.

"Gran? You okay?" I kneel next to her.

"I'm fine, Jimmy." Gran waves me away with one hand.

Great. Now she thinks I'm Gramps.

Gran straightens her shirt, picks up a stack of receipts from the box and drops them back in. "Just tidying up."

Van pulls her head out from the cupboard and says, "Good morning, Calvin." She passes me a cloth and points at the second cupboard. "A good grandson helps his *bà*."

"Sure." I take the cloth. Not that I get why we need to clean for Spader. "I just want to look something up online first."

Van nods. "Okay." She dips her cloth into the nearby bucket and then wrings it out.

I turn on the computer and pull up a chair.

"I remember when we first bought this place." Gran sighs. "We had loans from three different banks, and none of them knew about the others. That first year, we ate a lot of onion sandwiches."

"Onion sandwiches?" I make a grossed-out face. "Why?"

Gran startles, as if she hadn't realized she'd been talking. "Sorry?" Her clouded blue eyes find my face. "Oh, it's you, Calvin." She pats my leg. "Onions make a cheap meal. It was all we could afford."

"Oh." I frown. "Rough." I hope she won't be eating onion sandwiches again because Spader ripped her off.

I google Marshall's blog. When it starts to load, I stiffen, bracing for impact. What if Marshall wrote something terrible about me? What if he didn't write anything at all?

Seconds later, the headline stuns me. *Yo-Yo Genius.* Just like I predicted.

My skin prickles.

I glance at the photo of me with Eleanor, and then I skim the post: *Calvin Layne—yo-yo master or fortune-teller? There's no question that Layne can throw a yo-yo. He practically defies the principles of time and space. The question is: can he ascend into a Zen state that allows him to see the future?*

It goes on for a while, reviewing my shows and predictions. Then it says, *Based on what this blogger witnessed, Calvin Layne deserves the title Yo-Yo Prophet.*

"Whoa." I lean back in my chair. Even Marshall believes in the Yo-Yo Prophet.

"What is it, Calvin?" Van is at my shoulder.

"Uh, nothing. Just something about these yo-yo tricks I did," I say. "I can help you clean now." Marshall also posted a video of my performance, but I plan to watch it later, in private.

I turn off the computer and push in the chair. I start wiping down a cupboard, not with as much enthusiasm as Van, but it gets clean enough.

"So this deal with Spader...," I begin.

Gran is gazing into the box again, looking lost.

"The sale closes on Friday," Van says.

"In five days. I know." I think about the prediction I made earlier this morning that Spader's deal is too good to be true. "What do you know about this guy? I mean, why does Spader want to buy this place? Can he be trusted? People try to cheat all the time, you know." I leave out the bit about Gran being an easy target right now.

"Oh, Calvin." Van stops scrubbing. "We talked about this before. Your *bà* needs this sale."

"I know, but Gran should find the best deal, shouldn't she? Because if this deal sucks, you and I can take care of the shop until a new deal comes along. It's not like we're in a rush or anything. Maybe we should..." I trail off because Van has gone stiff, although her deep brown eyes are soft on me.

"It is time to tell him," she says to Gran.

Gran looks surprised, and then she nods. "It is." Her eyes seem clearer, like she's back from wherever she went.

"What's going on?" I glance back and forth between them, squeezing my cloth so tight that it drips water on my leg. "Tell me what?"

Van drops her cloth into the bucket. She settles back on her heels. "I have been trying to find a good time to tell you, but no time is right." She sighs. "I am moving to Vancouver. You know my daughter's baby will be born soon, and her son, Samuel, is only two. With two young ones, she will need my help, and I want to be close to them."

"But you can't!"

Van and Gran exchange looks. Gran grips one of my hands. Her fingers feel cold, frail.

"This is hard. I know." Van is wringing her hands. "For me too. That is why I did not tell you before. I wanted to, but...I just could not find the words. They"—she makes a fluttering motion with her hands—"flew away."

"But we need you too." My voice is too loud. "Can't someone else help your daughter?" Even as I say it, I realize how ridiculous it sounds.

Van shakes her head and looks away. "I have to go."

I'm trembling now. I guess I'm being selfish, not caring about her family, but I just can't help it.

Gran squeezes my hand. "That's one of the reasons I'm selling the store." Her voice is raspy, like how she gets before the coughing starts. "I can't run it without Van's help."

"I have already given notice to my landlord," Van says. "I leave at the end of June."

"In two weeks? But, Van!" I lean against the wall and rub my eyes. Is this really happening? Vancouver is on the other side of the country.

The bell over the front door rings as someone enters the store. I'm numb. I thump the back of my head against the wall.

Van leaps to her feet, saying, "Sorry, the door should be locked. We are…oh, hello, Mr. Spader."

Spader's face appears over the counter. I can see the disgusting little hairs inside his nostrils. What does he want?

"Mr. Spider." Gran struggles to stand.

I help her up.

"Mrs. Layne," he answers, bowing his head slightly. Spader's salt-and-pepper hair is freshly cut. His shirt is clean and wrinkle-free.

Gran brushes off her skirt. She muffles a cough with her hand.

I watch Spader carefully, hoping he'll slip up and expose whatever scam he's planning.

"I'm sorry to bother you on a Sunday," he says, "but I just happened to be driving by. Are we on track for next Friday?"

"Certainly. We're just clearing out a few things." Gran's voice is still raspy.

"Wonderful. And the apartment?"

"Yes?"

"You've found a new place to live?"

"To live?"

"A new home." Spader's nostrils flare. "Remember? We agreed that you would vacate the apartment by August first. I only ask because I know it can be hard to find good rental properties right now."

Gran stares blankly at Spader. I get a sinking feeling. Van looks grim.

"Please tell me you've been looking for a new home, Mrs. Layne." Spader raises his eyebrows.

"Well..." Gran is visibly shaking. She glances at Van. "I haven't found anything yet."

Van puts a hand on Gran's shoulder. "It is okay, Nancy. There is still time. We will find you a place."

A wicked cough erupts from Gran's throat. "Of course we will." Gran slumps as a coughing fit overtakes her.

She leans against the counter. Her face goes red. Her eyes water.

"Gran!"

"Mrs. Layne!"

Van and I both reach for an arm, but Gran's legs collapse, and she's falling, still coughing.

"No!" I yell.

Gran thuds to the floor, just missing the stool, clutching her chest. I'm tugging at her arm to ease her fall, but I only manage to collapse on top of her.

I leap off, afraid I've crushed her. Van and I kneel beside her.

"Gran?"

She hacks and splutters as we prop her up. Her face gets redder. She struggles for air. Her eyes shut. Tears stream down her cheeks. Spader towers over us.

There's a long moment when I'm holding my breath for Gran, as if it will help her catch hers. I can only hear Gran's cough, smell the dust and chemicals of the store, feel my heart hammering, my hand clenched around Gran's. I want to force her throat open, make her be okay.

One big cough and then Gran gasps in air. She moans. Her eyes open. They find me. "Richard?" she asks.

"Call the doctor," I tell Van. To Spader I say, "Leave us alone. I think you've done enough."

Gran's room smells worse than my locker at school.

The blind is drawn, although a crack of morning sunlight slices across the hardwood floor and up the pink and green floral wallpaper. I tiptoe from the door to her double bed. She's in a flannel nightgown, rolled on her side facing the wall, the faded pink covers tangled around her legs. Her breathing is heavy, rattling.

I stand there, watching her shoulder rise and fall. It's about all I've done for the last three days, other than take her to doctor appointments and worry about her. I've even missed two days of school so far, although I couldn't care less. Gran is more important.

The drawer of her night table is open, and photos lie scattered across the bed—pictures of Gramps and my father, and one of my mother as a girl in Vietnam. There's also a newspaper open to the classifieds. A few ads for apartments have been circled.

I frown. The doctor said she should be resting. He's going to run some more tests—try to figure out what's wrong with her—once she's stronger.

I turn to leave, trying to avoid the squeaky floorboards. Gran's steady wheeze grows louder, bubbling into a cough.

I turn back as she wakes, hacking. She rolls on her back and props herself up, coughing till her eyes stream with tears. The covers shift, and photos fall to the floor.

I hand her a tissue and pick up the photos. I wish I could do more. "You okay?" I ask, knowing she isn't.

She nods and wipes her eyes. Then she reaches out a shaking hand for the photos.

I pass them over. "You don't have to look for an apartment right now. Van has promised to help."

Gran sighs heavily. "I know." Her voice is rough. The skin on her face is sagging and gray. It scares me.

She glances at the photos, and her eyes glaze over. "I remember the day Richard got that bicycle. Red, it was, with a loud horn. Jimmy ran it over with the car that very night." She shakes her head, her lips curving up at the corners. "An accident, of course. Richard left it in the alley, right behind the car." She strokes the photo. "Remember how he cried? He was always so sensitive."

My father cried? "Gran, I wasn't even alive then."

"What?" Gran peers up at me, squinting as if she's trying to figure out who I am. "Calvin? Why aren't you in school?"

It's like she disappears and then comes back to me. And I never know when she'll go, or if she'll stay away for good. "I'm not going today."

"Because of me? You should go. Don't you have exams next week? You've missed two days this week already."

I blink, surprised. How does she know all that when she seems so out of it most of the time? "But the doctor said someone should—"

"Van's downstairs. She can help me out. Now go on." She sets her chin in the way that means she's serious.

I consider arguing, or just refusing, but it's not worth upsetting her. Anyway, I'd like to go, just to see if anyone at school has seen Marshall's blog post or the video. I could only bear to watch the video once—I looked so dorky. Some of the comments were okay, but what will people who know me think? My stomach knots. Most people think a yo-yo is just a toy.

"I'll be back right after school," I say. "And I'll tell Van to come up."

In a few minutes, I'm veering into the back of the shop, looking for Van.

Franco's at the steam press, looking bulky and tough even though he spends his time pressing clothes. His biceps ripple as he pulls the arm down on the press, trapping the clothes and releasing a cloud of steam. When he catches sight of me, his gaze falls heavy, and his face changes—downturned eyebrows and a pitying half smile.

I hold his gaze without smiling. I don't need his pity.

Lucy's blocking my way. She's short, round and red in the face, with a bundle of dark hair wound into a loose bun on top of her head.

"How are you doing, Mr. Calvin?" She grips my arm.

"Fine, Lucy. Where's Van?"

"I think she went out." Lucy wipes a damp hair off her forehead.

I stare her down. Her eyes shift sideways, which is a sure sign she's lying. But why?

I hear Van, talking loudly at the front counter. It's her telephone voice—the one she uses to be heard over the sound of the machines. She's been here so long that she sometimes yells into the phone even when the machines are quiet.

"I've got to go, Lucy." I pull my arm free.

"But Mr. Calvin—"

I push past her. Van is standing at the counter, phone to her ear, her back to me. The sun shines through the front window, giving her straight black hair a silver halo. As I near, I hear her shout, "I said Richard Layne. Do you know where he is?"

Suddenly my throat tightens. My stomach flips. She'll never find him. Because if he wanted to come home, he would. He knows where we are: right where he left us.

I exit through the back of the shop.

"Tell Van I'm at school," I say to Lucy and Franco. "Tell her to watch over Gran."

•••

I stop in front of the doors to the school and wipe my palms dry on my shorts. I peer through the narrow window.

No one's in the hall, or on the grounds. I've probably missed most of first period by now. I grab the door handle and then let go like it's electrified. What if everyone thinks yo-yos are lame? What if they laugh?

My head is buzzing. I scrunch up my toes inside my shoes and lean my forehead against the window.

Maybe I should wait till second period starts. I could sneak in when the hall gets crowded. I hate how everyone gapes at me when I come in late. I hate Ms. Friezen, the school secretary, who hands out hall passes along with endless lectures.

I peel my forehead off the window and reach into my pocket for one of my red yo-yos. What I need is some gravitational satisfaction before I face Ms. Friezen, Marshall, anyone. Or maybe I should just head home.

I turn to see this guy coming up the walk toward me.

He's in grade ten, I think. Blond hair in his eyes, baggy T-shirt, jean shorts, bright green Converse. He's working a yo-yo badly, like it's his first time.

I watch that yo-yo wobbling up and down the string like a drunk on a skateboard. My eyes see it, but my brain can't process it. This guy—older than me—is bringing a yo-yo to school? And he's worse at it than Gran would be? Talk about social suicide.

The guy looks up. His eyes widen when they land on me. "That you?" His yo-yo falls limp, flattens into a spin. "Calvin?"

I glance around. No one else is in sight. "Are you talking to me?"

He grins. "Sure. You are Calvin Layne, aren't you?"

"Uh, yeah."

He holds up his dangling yo-yo. It's a piece-of-crap wooden one, painted with orange flames. "Can you tell me how to work this thing?"

"Um. I guess." What's going on?

He wanders closer with his pathetic yo-yo. I explain to the guy—he tells me his name is Joseph—how to power throw and when to tug to make the yo-yo return. While he's working on that, I can't help tossing a few. The sun's beating down on us, and the smell of fresh-cut grass drifts on a warm breeze. Joseph is easygoing—he grins when his yo-yo spins outs. I'm starting to mellow, when I catch Joseph gaping.

"That's so cool!" he says. "Do that one with the flips again."

"You mean Buddha's revenge?" I start with a breakaway that leads into a one-and-a-half mount. Swing the yo-yo over my throwhand, landing it on the string on the opposite side. I bring my other hand underneath, making the yo-yo land on the string between my hands. Then I use my throwhand to land the yo-yo back on the string, let the yo-yo roll out to a trapeze and end with a Ferris-wheel dismount.

When I look up, Joseph's got this lopsided smile. "You're frickin' awesome!" He slaps me on the back.

A laugh bursts out of me, and my face gets hot.

"Show me more," Joseph says.

I shrug and let loose a few more moves. It's not showing off, really. He wants to see.

"Let me try that." Joseph lobs out his yo-yo and it flatlines. He can't even throw a sleeper. "I'm useless." He snorts. "Let's see that Buddha thing again."

I laugh. "You've got to start small. Buddha's revenge isn't for beginners."

I try to teach him a sleeper, but he keeps asking for Buddha's revenge. When I start to play it out for him one more time, I hear the squeak of hinges as the door to the school opens behind me. Focusing on my moves, I ignore it. When someone yanks me by the collar, I gag, stumbling backward into the school and jerking my yo-yo home before it crashes against the metal doorframe.

"Hey," I yell, twisting free.

"Where you been, Yo-Yo?"

"Rozelle." I face her—and Sasha and Annette. I don't exactly hate seeing Rozelle, but my throat hurts from where she yanked my collar. They're all looking as polished as usual, and I want to smack myself for noticing.

"I was gonna come lookin' for you." Rozelle is actually grinning, like she's sincere. "I mean, who would wanna miss this?"

"Miss what?" I glance around. My new best friend Joseph has trailed us in. Beside me, he's busy trying to throw a sleeper—and failing miserably. Other than us five, the hall is empty, the classroom doors closed.

"You." Rozelle smirks. "Goin' hard-core. Thanks to me."

Sasha rolls her eyes. Annette yawns, flips open her cell phone and examines the screen.

"Did anyone read the blog?" My stomach shrivels. "Do you know what they thought of it?"

"Yeah, they read the blog," Rozelle says, "and they watched the video. It got ten thousand frickin' hits on YouTube."

"What? Marshall posted it to YouTube?" My chest gets that tight feeling. "What were the comments?"

The buzzer goes for the end of the period. Classroom doors open. The hall floods with people.

A couple of guys do a doubletake when they see me.

"Is that him?"

I'm swarmed in seconds.

"Calvin, show us some tricks!"

"Yeah, I hear you're a genius."

Was that sarcasm?

They come at me like wolves at a dead lamb. Rozelle laughs.

"Let's go, Yo-Yo Prophet," some grade-twelve guy shouts as more people gather.

"Let's see how you do it!" someone yells.

"Give 'em that Buddha one!" Joseph says.

I take in the smiling faces of the people who usually ignore me. Now they're praising me, calling for a show. It's incredible. I feel like I can take on anything.

"Yeah, this is kickin'." Rozelle drapes an arm over my shoulder, and I don't flinch. "So enjoy it." She pushes me toward the crowd.

I see Geordie, who looks star-struck. Maybe I could have shown him my routine. A girl comes up and asks me for an autograph. I get this feeling of being airborne—of hovering in place like I'm about to take off.

I sign the front of the girl's binder, scan the faces of the kids clamoring to see me throw. It's okay with me if they never stop.

Sasha's standing back, scowling. Annette looks bored. I shrug them off and pull out my twin racers to throw my best show ever.

I'm tossing two-handed loops, flying high, setting everyone on fire, when Sasha steps too close.

"Watch out!" I yell, as I glimpse Mr. Davis, the principal, barreling toward us, probably to break up the party. He's got the sleeves of his dress shirt rolled up to his massive biceps. There's a frown on his face. Rumor has it that he used to be a pro-football player. Probably a linebacker.

Sasha's eyes flick to Mr. Davis before she flashes me a wicked grin, fakes a shriek and lets the yo-yo smack her beside her right eye.

"Ow!" She moans, clutching her eye and falling to one knee.

"Are you okay?" Annette lunges for Sasha, but Rozelle holds her back, her glare scorching.

My hands are fists around my yo-yos. I shut my eyes. Sasha's a venomous spider, and I'm a stupid fly.

"What's going on here?" Mr. Davis bellows.

My show ends as I'm hauled away by the collar for the second time that day.

My pockets are empty. My yo-yos have been imprisoned for the last hour in Mr. Davis's oversize desk. My hands ache to finish my last trick. Why did Sasha do this to me? Am I really that much of a threat?

I squirm in a hardback chair as Mr. Davis smoothes his tie against his shirt and sits in his cushioned leather chair. His chest muscles are barely contained by his shirt. He looks like a pro wrestler, or maybe a giant troll with hairy knuckles. As he rolls the chair closer to his desk, he runs a hand over his balding head and then frowns across at Gran and me. "Thanks for coming in, Mrs. Layne. I prefer to have serious conversations with a parent or guardian present. As for you, Calvin"—his eyebrows knot—"what do you have to say for yourself?"

"It's not my fault," I say. "Sasha stepped into my trick."

Gran purses her lips disapprovingly. She's pale, and there are dark circles under her eyes. It's my fault she's here when she should be home in bed.

Mr. Davis's endless forehead wrinkles. "You've had an hour to think about your actions, Calvin, and I had hoped you would use the time to seriously consider what you've done." He opens a desk drawer, plucks out my twin racers and dumps them on the desk, making me wince as they bang against each other. "Physical assault. Possession of weapons." He raises a finger for each of my crimes. "Even though this is your first offence, those are seriously inappropriate behaviors." He rests his hands on the desk.

I want to leap up and rescue my yo-yos. Instead, I sit on my hands and dig my nails into the fabric of the chair. "Yo-yos aren't weapons," I say, unable to keep quiet. Maybe Rozelle is rubbing off on me. Maybe I'm finally standing up for myself.

"No, they're not intended to be, but when you aim them at a fellow student, they become weapons."

"I didn't aim them at anyone!" I leap up. "She wanted to be hit. She did it on purpose!"

"Calvin!" Gran's voice is sharp. "What's got into you? You never get in trouble and now you talk back?" She stifles a cough. At least she's not calling me Richard.

I thump back into my seat. "But, Gran, you don't understand. She screamed before the yo-yo even hit her. I'm not making this up." Sasha set me up. Can't they see?

Mr. Davis shakes his head. "I can't force you to feel remorse, but I do hope that more time to reflect will help." He sighs as if he's deeply offended. "I'm going to suspend you from classes for the rest of the day, as well as for Thursday and Friday. Of course, you'll be permitted to sit your exams next week, so I suggest you arrange to get class notes from another student."

"He will." The veins in Gran's hands bulge as she grips the handle of her purse.

I slump as his words sink in. Suspended? Me? I can't believe it, although I'm guessing Sasha will be pleased. She gets attention while I get punished.

Mr. Davis continues. "And I must insist on a written apology to Sasha Reynolds."

"An apology!" I explode. "No way!"

"Calvin, stop!" Gran says, her chest gurgling.

I try to calm down.

"The safety of the students is my priority, Calvin," Mr. Davis says. "You have my decision. I suggest you consider the choices you made today—really think about your actions. I don't want a repeat of this situation." He stands, rattling the coins in his pocket. "I expect to see you first thing Monday morning in my office with that apology in hand."

"Okay," I mutter. It's not like I have a choice.

"Thank you, Mr..." Gran's voice trails off. She's probably forgotten his name.

I eye my yo-yos. "Can I have them back now?"

Before Mr. Davis can speak, Gran reaches an unsteady hand to sweep them off the desk and into her wide purse. She clicks the purse shut and tucks it under her arm. "I'll take care of them." She gives me a stern look.

I'm so thrilled to see them with Gran that I manage to nod repentantly at Mr. Davis on the way out.

"Sorry, sir," I say. I don't have to mean it.

"That's more like it." He bobs his head, the fluorescent lights reflecting off his shiny scalp. "Keep it up, Calvin, and you'll be back on track in no time." He shakes my hand, squeezing too hard.

As Gran and I are leaving the office, we bump into my two least-favorite teachers—Mr. Marnello and Ms. Kinsela. I cringe. If Ms. Kinsela ever got hold of my twin racers, I'd never see them again.

I try to steer Gran around them, but Mr. Marnello steps in my path.

"Calvin." His bushy mustache wriggles as he talks. "Why weren't you in math?"

I get the feeling that whatever I say will be wrong, just like in math class.

"I, uh, got suspended, Mr. Marnello." I duck my head, suddenly ashamed. Everyone will think that I did something wrong, that I deserve to be suspended. I stare at Gran's scuffed black shoes with the wide, clunky heels, wishing we were out of here.

"I'm not surprised," Ms. Kinsela says.

I glance up. What does she mean? I'm not that bad.

"Well, I am." Mr. Marnello turns to Gran. "Calvin always tries so hard in class. He's not afraid to answer questions."

Answer them wrong, I think. And math terrifies me. But I'm stunned. Mr. Marnello is on my side?

"How long will you be gone?" Ms. Kinsela's red hair is pulled back into a bun. It makes her skin look tight.

"Till Monday."

Her face falls—like she's actually disappointed.

"Why?" I have to ask.

"I heard about the"—she pauses to glance at Mr. Marnello and then at Gran—"incident with the yo-yo this morning. I had hoped you might do a yo-yo demonstration in my physics classes, but, with a student hurt and you suspended, it's impossible."

"You'd want me to come to a physics class?" I'm amazed. "Why?"

"Planes," she says. "A yo-yo operates on the principle of planes. You wouldn't be able to do complicated tricks if you didn't keep the yo-yo on a plane when you threw it."

"Oh," I say, not understanding a word.

"You see, the plane is formed by the yo-yo itself. When it's spinning, it has gyroscopic stability." Ms. Kinsela pretends to toss a yo-yo, which is too weird. "That's how the yo-yo stays in a line when you throw it." She goes on about inertia and spinning molecules. "My physics students would have enjoyed a demonstration."

"Maybe he could come in next year." Gran looks at me proudly. Her sweater has dipped off one shoulder and her dress sags. She's lost too much weight.

"That might be possible." Ms. Kinsela nods.

"I guess I could," I say, still surprised.

When Gran starts asking my teachers about my grades and the exams next week, I notice Rozelle down the hall, hanging around, probably waiting to hear what happened with the principal. I slip away from the adults.

"Three-day suspension," I tell Rozelle. "Because of Sasha."

Rozelle shrugs. "It's just school. Now, you get more time to practice."

"Yeah, I guess. But why did she do that?" I pace the hall. "I mean, she's always out to get me."

"Jealous, I guess," Rozelle says. "She thinks I spend too much time on you. Don't worry 'bout it."

"Why not?" I come to a sudden stop. "Are you going to make her pay for sabotaging my show?"

"I already took care of her. She won't pull that shit again." Rozelle grins, leans against a locker.

"What'd you do?" I ask. I'm imagining a fight behind the school—maybe a broken arm.

Rozelle shrugs again. "Let's just say I straightened her out. Listen, don't let her get to you. You're the man right now. They love you."

"Yeah, I guess you're right." They had still been cheering for me when Mr. Davis hauled me away. "But I wish—"

"We got bigger plans." Rozelle nudges me. "School's almost out. We should take the show to the streets this summer—maybe find a few carnivals or get into that busker festival downtown. I got us a street permit now, so the cops can kiss my—"

"How do you think of all this?" I shake my head, amazed. "You should do this for real, you know."

"Do what?"

"Manage talent."

Rozelle looks pleased. "You still don't get it." She gives me a friendly slap on the cheek. "This *is* for real."

Real? Even the predictions? I know what Rozelle would say. *Who cares? Just ride it as far as you can.* And maybe she's right.

Then Gran's beside me, looking exhausted as she extends a hand to Rozelle. "So nice to meet one of Calvin's friends. I'm his grandmother."

Rozelle raises one eyebrow, probably surprised by my white grandmother. "Hey." She shakes Gran's hand, introduces herself. They look odd together—Gran pale and tired, Rozelle dark and powerful.

Rozelle is saying, "I manage Calvin's shows. You should come see one. It's pretty cool."

"Well, I better get out of here," I say, breaking up the awkward party. I can just imagine what Gran thinks of Rozelle's low-cut shirt, jean miniskirt and combat boots, and I don't want Gran to embarrass me. "Suspended, you know."

Gran frowns. I guess it's not a joke to her. Me either, really. I've never been suspended before, and it doesn't feel so great.

Gran and I head down the hall, and I'm surprised when Rozelle strolls along with us, babbling about her plans for my summer, like she doesn't have a class to go to. Gran nods and asks questions, but I can tell she needs to lie down before she collapses. I speed up, hoping to end the conversation and get Gran home. I burst through the school doors, holding one open for Gran.

Outside, a cameraman and a female reporter wait at the sidewalk beside a white van from the local TV station.

"What's this?" Rozelle strolls out after Gran.

"That him?" The cameraman points at me. He's got messy brown hair and he's wearing an AC/DC T-shirt.

I stop abruptly. They're here for me?

The reporter glances up. "Are you Calvin Layne?" She's holding a microphone and wearing a pink jacket with black pants and high heels. "The Yo-Yo Prophet?"

"Oh, my!" Gran claps a hand over her mouth and chokes back a cough.

My heart races. How did they hear about me? Marshall's blog? Maybe YouTube? I glance questioningly at Rozelle, who looks as surprised as I am.

"Don't blow this, Yo-Yo," she whispers, elbowing me hard in the ribs, "or I'll knock you flat."

I elbow her back, just to show she can't push me around. "I can handle this."

Rozelle smirks, almost as if she's proud.

"I'm Calvin." I stroll across the dandelion-dotted grass toward the reporter, sweat beading on my forehead, trying to act confident.

Shafts of sunlight break through the leaves overhead. A breeze blows through my hair. Gran and Rozelle keep pace on either side—a heroic triangle with me at the center. As I near the sidewalk, a TV camera is shoved in my face. I grin into it, glad I remembered to gel my hair this morning.

"Okay, roll it," the cameraman says.

The reporter positions herself beside me, tosses back her long black hair and squares her shoulders at the camera, microphone in hand. "Roberta Chow reporting for Urban-TV Community News. We're here with Calvin Layne, also known as the Yo-Yo Prophet, a grade-nine student at Cliffdale High School. Sources say he earned his street name by making accurate predictions while performing yo-yo tricks. Can you give us a demonstration, Calvin?" She aims the microphone at my face.

I'm a little thrown by how aggressive the reporter is, but I recover quickly. "Sure I can," I say, glancing at Gran. She gives me a grim look—probably to remind me that I'm still in trouble—and then opens her purse and hands me my twin racers. Rozelle gives me a thumbs-up.

I go full-out, beginning with ten crisscross loops and shifting into double vertical punches over my head. I finish with multiple milk-the-cows in front of me.

The cameraman records it all, while the reporter bombards me with questions. How long have I been yo-yoing? Have I won any competitions? How many predictions have I made? How accurate have my predictions been?

I answer the best I can while I stay focused on my tricks.

The school buzzer goes for lunch. Soon, people are pouring out the doors, and I'm surrounded by cheering as I do a sword-and-shield trick.

"As you can see," says the reporter, "this kid is a big hit!"

The cameraman pans the crowd—Joseph applauding and grinning; Geordie, a head taller than the rest, looking shocked at what I can do; Rozelle nodding; Marshall snapping photos of the event; musclehead jocks and rapper-wannabes cheering side by side. The camera returns to me as I impress with a circular fountain of two-handed trajectories, starting out nearly horizontal and ending fully vertical.

Gran retreats to the bench by the bus stop when a coughing fit overtakes her. She waves to show me she's okay. I should get her home, but I need to rule this show.

I rock one trick after another, even find new combinations that I'd never tried before.

As I'm starting into a windshield-wiper trick, the reporter asks, "Have you heard of Black Magic?"

"What?" I'm throwing a breakaway with one hand and a reverse breakaway with the other to wipe the windshield.

"He won the World Yo-Yo Contest a few years back. He lives here now."

"I've seen him online." I'm an ace, playing it up for the camera. Blood screaming through my veins, the yo-yos screaming through my fingers.

"Well, the talk is starting—Yo-Yo Prophet versus Black Magic. Who do you think would win a spin-off?"

I switch into a looping arm wrap. "I would, of course." No one can touch me now.

"Is that a prediction?" the reporter says it like a challenge.

"Sure is." I'm invincible. Solid gold. I can beat anyone, anytime.

I finish my show without interruptions. Sasha left ages ago, and Annette is nowhere in sight.

Afterward, the reporter pulls me aside. "That was better than I expected. You're all right." She smiles without showing her teeth.

"He's more than all right." Rozelle saunters over. "He's the frickin' best."

"And who are you?" The reporter's eyes rake over Rozelle, sizing her up.

"I'm his manager," she says, "and we need to talk 'bout how I can get a copy of that video."

On the subway ride home, the walls of the tunnel flash by at dizzying speed. Gran and I share a bench. My hands twitch in my lap as if they're still working tricks. Gran leans her head against the Plexiglas window. She's tilted away from me, like a car with two flat tires on one side.

I know I should be worried about her, but I'm too excited. "So what'd you think of the Yo-Yo Prophet, Gran?" I can barely stay seated. I bet she thought I was awesome.

"I think you need to study for exams," she says.

"But—"

"And you need to keep your yo-yos out of the school." Gran coughs hard, holding her chest till she catches her breath. She purses her lips and shuts her eyes.

Then I realize how hard she's been working to hold it together for me—trying to be strong because she thinks I messed up, even though I didn't. It's all because of Sasha. I grit my teeth, reaching into my pocket to finger a yo-yo.

The subway rattles across a track connection, rocking us in our seats. The car smells faintly of garbage and sweat. Across from us, a tough guy dressed in gangsta gear sits next to a businessman in a suit. They look as mismatched as Gran and me.

"I have no problem with you playing this Yo-Yo Prophet." Gran's eyes open. "And I don't believe you'd harm a young girl on purpose. But you do need to be more careful. You need to keep those yo-yos under control."

"That's what I do best." I can't help but smile. "No worries, Gran."

Gran studies me with her eyebrows raised before she leans her head against the window again and closes her eyes.

When we get home, we head straight upstairs, skipping the shop and the status report from Van. Gran falls into bed. In the living room, I notice that someone—probably Van—has started to pack Gran's collection of plates. The walls are mostly bare, with round patches of unfaded paint to mark where each plate once hung. I guess we really are moving, even if we haven't found a place yet.

I switch on the TV and flip to the local channel, wondering when Urban-TV News will come on. A boring talk show is playing, so I press *Mute* and stare at the screen. When I can't sit still any longer, I pace the room, weaving among the half-filled packing boxes, thinking through what happened at school. Not my typical day—that's for sure. First I get suspended, and then I'm a celebrity, a hero. The kind of guy that always gets the girl. As if.

Rozelle says it's only the beginning.

My hands are jittery. I pull out my yo-yos and replay my favorite moves.

When there's a knock at the door, I hurry to open it before the noise wakes Gran. Lucy and Franco, Gran's workers from the shop, are outside. Lucy's standing on the metal landing, her hands clutched together. Franco is one step behind her, shifting uncomfortably from foot to foot. I can't remember them ever coming upstairs before.

"What's wrong?" I ask in a whisper. Gran's room is just across the hall.

"It's Van." Lucy stumbles over her words. Franco's mustache is twitching. "She had to go."

"Go where?" Tension rises through my stomach to my chest, tightening my throat so my voice comes out in a squeak. "Where did she go?"

The telephone rings.

"Just a minute," I say, leaving them standing awkwardly at the door while I run to the living room for the phone, hoping Gran won't wake.

The TV is still on mute, displaying images of silky hair for some shampoo ad. When I pick up the phone, I hear Van's voice through the receiver before it's even to my ear.

"Hello? Hello?" she says.

"Van? Where are you?"

"I am at the airport," she says. "My flight will be going in a few minutes. I keep calling and calling, but you take so long at school. Is everything okay?"

"Yeah, sure." Her urgent tone gets me on edge. "Why are you at the airport? You're not leaving till the end of June, right?" She can't leave me yet.

"I have a change in plans. My daughter, she is in the hospital. She went into labor," she says.

"The baby is coming? But it's not time." My heart contracts. I'll never see Van again. Never get her back. She'll be so busy…

"Yes, it is too soon for the baby to be born." Van's loud voice startles me. "They managed to stop the labor, but my daughter will need to stay in the hospital until it is safe for the baby to be born. That is why I am needed as soon as possible. Someone must watch Samuel, since his father has to work."

"I understand," I say, keeping my voice calm, even though I want to scream. How can she leave me now? With Gran sick? Who will find us a new place to live?

Maybe we can use Van's place. "Is your apartment rented yet?" I ask.

Van sighs. "Yes. the landlord already rented it, although it would have been too small for you and your *bà*. I did leave a list of apartments for rent on the front counter in the shop. Your *bà* should be able to find something soon." She mutters something in Vietnamese. "So sorry. I feel so bad. I should not leave you with this mess. And your *bà* sick!"

"It's okay, Van." I try to lie well. "Gran and I will be fine. Soon we'll be calling you from our new place." I grip the phone tighter. "We'll probably get a house," I add.

"You always take good care of your *bà*," Van says. "But everyone needs help sometimes. That is why I asked Lucy and Franco to watch out for you. Lucy will bring supper each night, and Franco lives nearby, if you need anything else. They will even help you pack."

“Thanks, Van,” I say, even though I’m planning to keep Lucy and Franco out of my business. They’ve both worked for Gran a long time, but they’re not like Van.

I write down her daughter’s phone number and then wish her luck.

“Goodbye, Calvin. Don’t forget to bolt the door to the alley at night,” Van says.

I hang up.

The apartment is silent.

At the door, Franco clears his throat.

Ignoring him, I gaze stupidly at the living-room walls, remembering how customers would sometimes mistake Van for my mother. And suddenly, I hate the empty walls. I snatch a newspaper-wrapped plate from a nearby box, wanting to rehang all the royal porcelain faces.

Maybe then I won’t feel so alone.

I unwrap the plate. A weak-chinned Prince Charles offers no comfort.

When Lucy and Franco enter the living room, I jump. I’d forgotten that I left them standing at the door.

I return Charles to his box and then shoo Lucy and Franco out of the apartment as fast as I can, hating their sad eyes and promises to help. When they’re gone, I flop onto the couch and stare at the mute TV. My brain’s humming and my body’s wired like a radio receiver ready to pick up signals from outer space, but I can't move. I can't even grip a yo-yo.

When I hear Gran stir, I heat up some tomato soup. She eats propped up on pillows and then falls asleep again. I let my soup grow cold. The smell of it disgusts me, although I could sure go for a bowl of my mother's noodle soup right now.

When the news comes on, I watch myself on screen, heart pounding. The reporter calls me a "local sensation" and says I "capture the spirit of street performers in the city."

My hands come alive first. I'm standing, miming my moves, unable to stay still, reliving the glory. It's just a community program, but it feels like *Entertainment Tonight*.

If I shut my eyes, I can still feel the crowd urging me on.

•••

By Thursday, I'm going multiball, trying to keep everything in play. I study math until my brain hurts, and then I start packing the pieces of my life with Gran into cardboard boxes. When Gran finally wakes, I get breakfast, making her promise to rest between the phone calls she's making to find us a new place. Van can't help us find an apartment from Vancouver. I go downstairs to help out in the shop. I take in clothes that will become Spader's responsibility. I try to study science between customers. And I run up to check on Gran every so often.

I almost wish Rozelle were here, forcing Sasha and Annette to pack or write my study notes. But I don't want them in my apartment, going through my drawers or Gran's old photos, mocking everything.

Near the end of the day, Van calls to check on us. I promise that everything is fine, and she tells me how happy she is to see her daughter and grandson. "The nurses take good care of my daughter, and Samuel is—how do you say it?—a little angel." Van's voice softens when she talks about Samuel. "When he visits his mother in the hospital, he sings to the baby in her belly. In four more weeks, it will be safe for the baby to be born." Van is breathless and in a hurry, so we don't talk long.

Lucy, Franco and I clean up the shop for the last time. I straighten the few things left on the front desk. I'm going to miss the computer, but it belongs to the shop. Lucy and Franco tidy the back. I won't really miss working in the shop or the smell of chemicals or the dust, but I'm sad for Gran, especially since she's not even here to say goodbye. Lucy and Franco have to find new jobs, since Spader is hiring his own staff.

Just as I'm powering down the computer, the bell over the front door jingles and Spader walks in. He's fumbling with two large signs mounted on white foam backing. He's all elbows and knees. "Calvin." He nods.

"It's only Thursday," I say. I still can't forgive him for upsetting Gran. He practically made her collapse.

"Yes, I know," Spader answers mildly. "Is your grandmother available?"

He leans the signs against the wall. One says in bold green lettering *Chemical-Free Dry Cleaning*, but it's the other one that irks me: *Under New Management*.

I fold my arms across my chest. "She's sick. The doctor says she has to stay in bed."

"I'm sorry to hear that. I had hoped she would be better by now." He strokes his neatly trimmed goatee. "And her next in charge—Van, I think it is? May I see her?"

"You can"—I narrow my eyes—"with a five-hour flight."

"I beg your pardon?" Spader's starting to get huffy. "I don't understand."

"She's in Vancouver." I shrug and slide into the chair in front of the computer, even though it's off. I pretend to type, like I have something important to do. "You'll have to deal with me."

Spader goes silent, and I can feel his eyes on me. I wish I were wearing a better T-shirt—at least a clean one—and that I'd put gel in my hair. I wish I could make my hands stop trembling over the keys.

"In that case, please tell your grandmother that I'll speak with her another day."

I meet Spader's eyes, which are steel blue. "Unless she's resting," I say. I keep my voice strong. I won't let him upset Gran again.

"Of course. I don't want to intrude." Spader motions to his signs. "In the meantime, do you mind if I leave these window signs here? It will save me lugging them home and back again."

"Well..." I love that he has to ask my permission. "I guess I'll allow it." I make my face go stony.

"Thank you, Calvin."

When Spader leaves, I bolt the door. He won't get close to Gran if I can help it.

On Monday at school, even the coolest grade twelves ask me for predictions. The power of YouTube, I guess. Joseph follows me around at lunch, asking me to teach him tricks. Geordie is happy to let me copy his notes from the last few days of classes; he acts like I'm some kind of celebrity.

"Why didn't you tell me you could do this?" he asks.

I shrug. "Guess I didn't know if you would like it."

"What are you talking about?" He gestures with his oversize hands. "You're awesome. Predicting the future is even better than reading minds. And it's so cool how it works with the yo-yo." He nods and looks thoughtfully into the distance. "It makes me think about yo-yos differently. They're like"—he pauses—"this source of untapped power."

I feel so good that I don't even mind handing my written apology to Mr. Davis.

Before my math exam, Mr. Marnello asks with a wink, "Any predictions about how well you'll do, Calvin?"

"I'll do okay, Mr. Marnello." I smile. On the weekend, I predicted that I'd get a B, which is pretty good, for me.

"I hope so."

When I bump into Marshall, he won't stop talking about the Urban-TV piece.

"I can't believe they picked up the story!" He tucks a strand of pink hair behind his ear. "I mean, I sent them a link to my blog, but I never thought they'd do anything with it. Do you think they liked it? Maybe I should send them more of my work."

"Course they liked it," Rozelle interrupts our conversation. "That's why you're gonna build us the official Yo-Yo Prophet blog, Marshall. You get to be our exclusive online reporter." She slaps Marshall on the back, and he grins.

Over the next week, between exams, Rozelle has me performing all over the city. I perform new and improved yo-yo tricks and spout one prediction per show.

I predict a man with stooped shoulders will find his lost cat, a guy about my age will pass his science exam and a woman with large teeth will break up with her boyfriend. They're not huge, world-changing predictions, but people like them. Rozelle carefully records each prediction, and she collects my cash in her red plastic bucket. She assigns Annette to work the music box and puts Sasha behind the video camera, with her two fading bruises—the one beside her right eye where my yo-yo hit her and the larger one on her left eye, supplied by Rozelle. I can't stay mad at Sasha when her eyes look like that.

Meanwhile, Marshall creates the Yo-Yo Prophet blog, complete with videos and photos from my performances, my Urban-TV interview, reports about my latest predictions and music supplied by Teknonaut. It's unreal, like a dream that might fade any minute.

•••

At the end of June, when my last exam is finally over, I celebrate with yet another performance—this time down at Harbourfront. The girls and I end up on the walk beside the lake, near the dock for the local cruise boats. I'm wearing baggy red shorts and a black T-shirt with

Yo-Yo Prophet on it in psychedelic lettering. I'm still trying to get used to the red streaks Rozelle put in my spiked hair.

I leap onto our makeshift stage—a few upside-down crates. I plan to impress the heck out of a crowd of tourists and office workers who are snatching a few summer rays. I toss double-handed and blindfolded, just for kicks. I send my red racers in loops under one leg and then the other, never slowing the pace, alert for reactions from the crowd.

"Whoa, I wanna see that again," some guy says.

My smile could crack my face in half. I can almost forget about Gran's illness, and how she hasn't yet found us a new place to live.

"Aw, that was sick." The girl sounds about my age, and if her body is as sexy as her voice, I can't wait to see her.

The music—courtesy of Rozelle's brother—sends a techno beat pounding through my chest. The sun toasts my face and shoulders. My yo-yos slice the air like a pair of medieval Japanese swords. I'm so frickin' amazing, I even impress myself.

I finish with crisscross punching bags and then call my twin racers home. I whip off my blindfold—a black and white silk scarf that Rozelle bought—and toss it like I couldn't care less where it lands. Rozelle snatches it up and pockets it.

"Yo, all!" Rozelle calls. People at the outdoor café lean in to listen, while Annette cuts the music. "My boy here is the Yo-Yo Pro-phet!" She raises her arms, making peace signs with both hands. "Not only can he yo," she bellows, "he'll tell ya how to go."

People laugh at her lame rapper imitation. I break into a series of double loops to carry me through Rozelle's chatter.

"This boy can give you the dope." She struts like she's in a music video. "Your own personal hor-o-scope."

Rozelle looks good in hot-pink leggings with a black sequined top that glitters in the sun. I scan the crowd for the girl with the fantastic voice.

"So step up if you wanna know"—Rozelle gestures at the crowd—"the way your future is gonna flow." She points to me with both hands and then steps away with a flourish.

On Rozelle's cue, Annette starts the music up again, at a lower volume this time so the crowd will be able to hear my Yo-Yo Prophet wisdom. A few people meander up, and Rozelle chats with them, one by one, since she likes to screen them—find one dramatic question for me to answer. But today, I'm impatient for the fun to begin. I decide to warm up the crowd with a few samples.

“Hey, people,” I say, breaking into around-the-worlds with one hand and crossover loops with the other. “Let me show you how it works.” I’m revving up my engine, getting ready to receive the visions.

“Stop it, Yo-Yo,” Rozelle says. “That ain’t a good idea.”

I ignore her. Who’s in charge here anyway?

I close my eyes, relax my neck and shoulders, even though I’m still tossing out my twin racers. I soak in the heat of the sun, the sounds and smells around me, till I swear I can taste the coffee-scented air from the café. The music takes me deeper inside, hypnotizing me with the steady rhythm, and my yo-yos become more than just plastic, stainless steel and string. When I toss them out, it’s like I’m freeing them, releasing good vibrations into the air that eventually rebound back to me. Like I’m in my body yet riding those pulsing vibrations at the same time.

When I reach a Jedi-like state, I open my eyes and let them skim over the crowd, sensing my way, until they land on Sasha, filming my show.

I nod in her direction. “I predict…” I pause dramatically as people crane to look at Sasha. “I predict she is filming yet another Yo-Yo Prophet YouTube hit.”

Sasha's face appears over the camera long enough to grimace at me and then at Rozelle. Her makeup covers most of the bruising.

I grin, catching sight of a gorgeous girl who just has to own that voice I heard before. She's got these enormous slate-gray eyes and soft blond hair that falls in loose waves to her shoulders. As she lifts her hair off the back of her neck with both arms, she smiles in this sexy way that heats me up.

Whoa. I thunk one yo-yo home and then the other. "I predict you," I point at her, my blood pounding, "are going to fall for a short Asian-Canadian guy."

The crowd laughs—they're on my side. I catch Rozelle scowling at me, but I don't care what she thinks. The girl's smile is smooth and easy.

I toss out my yo-yos again and crank into a double staircase to keep the groove. The sky is brilliant blue, while the lake glows green with sunlight riding the waves.

When Rozelle announces it's time for my big prediction, people at the café shuffle their chairs for a better view. I break into inside loops with one hand and reach-for-the-moons with the other.

On Rozelle's signal, a willowy woman—maybe twenty-five years old—flounces toward me. She moves like a ballerina, with her toes pointed out, and she beams first at me and then at the audience.

The crowd goes quiet, like it's holding its breath. I hear the waves break against the docks. I can tell why Rozelle chose this woman—the crowd seems to like her.

"I'm getting married next month—on August twentieth. It's a Saturday." Her eyes flip to a guy who's seated at a table outside the café. She waves to him, and a few people laugh. He waves awkwardly back. "So I want to ask you to predict the impossible." Her face becomes serious. "We're having this outdoor wedding in a park by the lake, so I'm really worried about the weather. There can be huge thunderstorms in August, and I have to know: Will the weather spoil our wedding? Should I have a backup plan?" She clasps her hands together and sends me a pleading look.

I focus on her question while spinning loop-the-loops—till the answer washes over me. "It may rain a bit," I say with confidence, "but it won't ruin your wedding."

The crowd applauds.

"I hoped you would say that!" The woman kisses both my cheeks, and I grin.

Rozelle works the crowd for donations to the "Yo-Yo Prophet fund," while Annette writes down the woman's info so Marshall can keep track of the prediction on my blog. So far, Marshall reports I have a one-hundred-percent accuracy rate, although I haven't yet proven I can beat Black Magic in a duel. Once this latest prediction comes true, Rozelle will be bragging that I can even predict the weather.

Rozelle pulls out a secondhand yo-yo and announces it's challenge time—where anyone can try to beat me at a trick—either the longest sleeper or the most consecutive loops.

Of course, it's a joke, because I can easily beat anyone. But people seem to like to be defeated by me, so I let them try. I even pretend to almost fail, every now and then.

When I call it quits, Rozelle tells the crowd where they can download Teknonaut songs. I've got to give her credit—she's always looking out for her brother. I have the usual group of keeners around me, praising my show and asking questions about how to yo-yo. Then—this is the best part—the gray-eyed girl poses with me as her friend takes a photo with her camera phone.

Our arms touch when she slides up against me, and my skin sizzles. Her hair smells like heaven. She's the perfect fit—a bit shorter than me—and her long blond hair falls against my shoulder.

"When's your next show?" she asks, her voice sweet and low in my ear.

"Uh..." I momentarily forget how to speak. "You can...check my blog for my next performance," I tell her.

"I'll be there," she breathes, "wherever it is."

I'm suddenly floating above the ground.

Then she leaves, swinging her hips in this slinky summer dress, glancing back at me before she disappears behind a hot-dog cart.

The crowd clears. Rozelle, Annette and Sasha gather around. I'm still pumped with adrenaline.

Sasha's looking sullen in all black—ripped jeans and a skintight top. She's shooting daggers my way. I'm sure she's still trying to plot my downfall.

Annette's in plaid short-shorts, bouncing at Rozelle's elbow. "How'd I do, Roz? I did it just like you said."

Rozelle is scowling at me, but she nods at Annette, who shoots Sasha a smug glance.

"If that video ain't top-notch, you'll be sorry," Rozelle says to Sasha, and I wonder what has set Rozelle off this time—we had such a great show.

"I told you I'd do it, so get off my back," Sasha yells, which does nothing to improve Rozelle's mood. Sometimes I wonder why those two are friends.

"And you," Rozelle growls at me, one hand on her hip. "What's up with makin' predictions I don't authorize?" She adjusts her tank top, but I refuse to get distracted.

"What do you care?" I fire back, tired of her random mood swings. "It's not like you're the talent, Roz. You're just a manager."

Rozelle's cheeks go burgundy. "You ain't nothin' without me."

Sasha snickers.

"Since when do you call her Roz?" Annette steps between us. "Only her friends call her that."

I ignore Annette and lock eyes with Rozelle. "Why do you always talk like you've got a grade-two education?" I ask. "Do you have to say *ain't* all the time?"

Rozelle's eyes are scorching. She pushes past Annette, one fist ready, the bucket of cash swinging from her other hand. "I'm gonna pound you till you can't stand up." Her breath is hot and sour.

I remember all the times she's threatened me—that first time after math class when I accidentally bumped into her, after my first show when she took half my earnings. Over and over again, she's bossed me around, made demands.

"What? You're going to harm your star?" I flip a yo-yo between us with a power throw, barely missing her knee.

She flinches. I let the yo-yo smack hard into my palm and then yank the bucket from her grip. "I'll divide up the money. You can get your cut later."

Annette gasps. Sasha chuckles. Rozelle's eyes bulge like she's going to explode.

I walk away, swinging the bucket.

The world is spinning at the end of my string, and I'm not about to let go.

The first thing Spader does when he takes over the shop is put up his new window signs. I get mad every time I read *Under New Management*—it's like he's bragging that he's better than Gran. Sure, she sometimes miscounted the change or confused an order, but her customers loved her, even gave her Christmas gifts.

Spader hires two guys to replace the sign over the blue-and-white-striped awning. *Queen's Eco Dry Cleaning*, it reads now. It may only be a small change, but it feels huge to me. Like Gran is already forgotten.

Changes are happening inside the shop too. From the apartment upstairs, we hear the screech of heavy machines grinding across the floor tiles, and we see the truck in the back alley delivering new machines—like Gran's old ones aren't good enough. Even the smell of the place changes. I'd kind of gotten used to the chemical smell that leached through the floorboards of the apartment. The new *perfume-free scent* that Spader is advertising is lame.

But the worst part is that we haven't got a new apartment, never mind a house with a garden. It's not about the money—with the sale of the business, Gran says we'll be fine. There are some nice places available for September first, but because Gran left it so long, all she has managed to find for August 1 is a room in a boardinghouse without our own kitchen and bathroom, or a termite-infested dump over a nightclub. And each time we make the trek to check out a place, Gran becomes more of a wreck—coughing, clutching my arm and complaining of lower back pain so much that, about a week after my Harbourfront performance, I take her to the doctor again. Not that Spader cares about her health; he just wants us out by the end of the month.

So when I head home from the drugstore with a new prescription for Gran's pain, I'm already pissed at Spader.

I see him inside the store, bent over like a pretzel to remove Queen Elizabeth II's photo from the window, and anger curls into a tight knot in my stomach. I can't let it go.

Yeah, the poster is cheesy, faded and out-of-date, but it's like Gran is being deposed. Like Spader is the new monarch. Maybe he should post a photo of himself so we can bow down to him.

I can't watch Spader peeling the tape off the window, bending the photo back as if he doesn't care if it tears. I yank open the familiar shop door and march in. An electronic bell sounds; he's ripped out Gran's metal bell over the door too.

"What are you doing?" I demand.

Spader glances up. "Oh, hello, Calvin. How's your grandmother?"

"As if you care!"

He straightens. His long fingers release the photo, leave it dangling half off the window. "I'm sorry?"

"Are you?" My voice is loud. "As if you don't know what you've done, what you're doing right now." I point to the curling poster.

Two men emerge from between the racks of plastic-wrapped clothes. One man has a shaved head. The other has bleached-blond, short-cropped hair.

"Even Gran's staff wasn't good enough for you," I yell. I know that Franco has found work in a sock factory, but Lucy is still looking.

"Calvin, maybe you should sit down." Spader motions to a row of cushy chairs lining the far wall. "Then we can talk."

"I don't want to sit."

The two men weave toward us through the clothes.

Spader waves them back, like I'm no threat, which makes me even madder. The men melt away into the racks of clothes. "Really, Calvin, you need to calm down."

I notice yet another sign on the wall: *Non-toxic Dry Cleaning—The Green Alternative.*

"You're mocking her." I stab a finger at the sign. "Like your ways are so much better."

Spader glances at the sign. "That? It's just advertising. I want to let people know about my methods. Some dry-cleaning chemicals are quite harmful. People want non-toxic alternative."

"Should we also let everyone know that you'll kick us out at the end of the month, even if we can't find a decent place to live?"

"But I—"

"Do you know how sick she is?" I grip the plastic drugstore bag, my fingernails digging into my palm.

"She shouldn't be out of bed, except to go to the doctor, but you've got her hiking all over the city to find us a new apartment!"

"I'm sorry to hear that. It was not my intention to—"

"If you really were sorry, you wouldn't make us leave."

"But, Calvin, it was your grandmother's decision to give up the apartment as of August first, so I signed a lease agreement with new tenants—"

"Who cares about your tenants? What about Gran?" I march to the door and swing it open, making the electronic bell sound again. "I always knew you would screw her over."

I slam the door. The glass rattles in its frame. Through the window, I see Spader staring after me, openmouthed.

My chest is bursting as I turn away.

I march around to the alley and up the stairs to the apartment to take care of Gran. I give her the medicine and a glass of water. I head to the kitchen to heat up the macaroni casserole Lucy delivered—she's still bringing supper each day, the way she promised. I also make Gran a cup of the Vietnamese green tea my mother got her hooked on.

When I have the supper tray loaded, I carry it into Gran's room and set it on the night table. With her pale skin and white hair against the rose-colored pillowcase,

Gran looks ghostly, although her eyes seem clear and focused.

"I heard yelling from downstairs," she says. "Is everything is okay?"

"Everything is fine." I sit on the bed and pass her a cup of tea. It's in a William-and-Kate souvenir wedding mug—only half full so she won't spill. "I was just talking to Spader."

"Talking? Then who was yelling?" She takes the mug from me. "Calvin, I know you've been skeptical of Mr. Spider, but he really has been wonderful to us. No one else was interested in buying this place, and his offer was generous. I hope you didn't upset him."

I can't believe her. "Don't worry about Spader." I pat her leg through the blanket. "Just get better."

The lines on Gran's forehead furrow deeper. "I wish I could," she says. She sips from the mug, her anxious eyes watching me over the rim.

•••

After Gran goes back to sleep, Van calls. She's been calling every day or two to check up on us.

"Calvin, how are you?" she says in Vietnamese. "How is your *bà*?"

"I'm fine, Van," I say, smiling at the sound of her voice. "And Gran is too." I try to sound convincing. "I'm taking good care of her."

"And you have a place to live?"

"Uh, almost. We'll sign a lease soon." I hope. I don't want her to worry. I tell her about Gran's new pain medicine, and even about my Yo-Yo Prophet blog, which she promises to look at. "How's your family?" I ask.

Van tells me that in about two more weeks it will be safe for the baby to be born. She says that Samuel has been drawing pictures for the baby. Then Van says goodbye, promising to call soon.

The silence closes in on me when I hang up, suspended in the air like a bad stink.

I wander into the living room. There's a pile of cardboard boxes along one wall, and no plates left on the discolored walls. I turn on the TV for company and to dull the ache in my chest. I should do some more packing, but instead I push the couch back and hurl some long loops since there's no china left to hit. When I've relaxed a bit, I work out the kinks in some of my more challenging tricks. I make a few predictions for myself: Will we find a new apartment? Yes. Will Gran get better? Yes. Will the gray-eyed girl be at my next show? Yes.

I let out a long sigh and tell myself that I've got everything under control.

There's a knock at the door—hammering, really—and I rush to it, cursing whoever is threatening Gran's rest. I open the door and step out, shutting it behind me. Rozelle stands on the metal landing, glowering.

"Shhh." I frown. "My grandmother's sleeping."

"Well, we got a schedule to work out." She curls one side of her lip, and I think how much prettier and nicer the gray-eyed girl is. "Unless you *ain't*"—she emphasizes the word—"got use for your manager no more."

I hold her gaze. We're face to chest on the landing with no room to move. "Sure, I like what you do for me," I say. "What's the plan?"

Her eyes smolder, but she gets to business. "First, we got this duel between you and Black Magic. I got it arranged for Saturday, three days from now, at four o'clock in Dundas Square. I even got that reporter comin'." She glares as if daring me to challenge her.

"Not bad." I nod slowly, not wanting to show her how excited I am. Then I add, "At least we know that I'll win the duel—since I predicted it."

Rozelle raises one eyebrow. "I also got you into the busker festival later this summer," she continues, her voice smug, "which sure weren't easy."

"Even better." I lean back against the railing. "You're doing all right."

"All right?" Rozelle's face turns red and her jaw tightens.

"Yeah." I shrug. "I mean, sometimes you forget whose show it is, but you do a good job, most of the time."

"You ungrateful turd!" Her nostrils flare like some wild horse in a western movie. "I update your image! Buy you new clothes! Get you gigs! Set you up right! And you say I'm doing *all right*?"

"Relax, Rozelle," I say.

"I ain't gonna relax. I'm gonna tell you how it is." She leans in, flattening me against the railing. "The manager is in charge of the money. The manager says what goes down."

"Is that what this is about? The money?" I try not to smile, knowing that it will drive her mental, but Rozelle has been yanking my strings from the beginning, and I like that I can make her crazy. "I've got it in my room. I didn't spend any, although I could have. After all, I made it."

"We made it." She pokes a finger into my chest.

I can't help grinning. "If it will make you feel better," I say, "I'll give you your cut now."

"You better!" Rozelle raises a fist, as always. "And you better believe that I'm collectin' the money in tomorrow's show. Because that's what managers do."

I ignore her fist. "As long as you remember who's in charge."

She narrows her eyes, her face in mine. "You think you can cross me? I made you the Yo-Yo Prophet, and I can bring you down. You couldn't get a gig without me."

"And you couldn't make money without me," I say. "Now, wait here while I get your cut."

I wake up, curled in a ball, protecting my head with my hands.

In my dream, I was about to battle Black Magic. We were on a stage in Gran's living room with her royal plates, figurines, cups and mugs arranged around us. People crowded one end of the room, with more pushing in from the hall. The gray-eyed girl was there, smiling at me. When I threw my first loop, I smashed Gran's rare George V coronation plate. "No," I yelled, as the plate fractured. I fought to stop throwing, but my hands wouldn't obey. Again and again, I destroyed her collection—the Queen Elizabeth II commemorative tankard, the Charles-and-Diana wedding teapot—shattering them with my yo-yos, crying out with each hit. Bits of china rained down. The gray-eyed girl screamed. Rozelle laughed hysterically. Black Magic didn't seem to notice. He threw an awesome routine while I demolished Gran's entire collection like a crazed ninja.

I sit up, trembling, and wipe imaginary slivers of china from my hair.

I glance around. I'm on the living-room couch. The sun is pouring in the windows, baking the cardboard boxes and barren walls. It must be almost noon. Did I fall asleep here last night?

I rub my eyes, confused.

Then I remember it's Saturday. Today I duel Black Magic.

My stomach knots.

Why am I nervous when I predicted what will happen? I will out-yo-yo Black Magic. The gray-eyed girl will come. It has to happen that way, doesn't it?

I stumble past Gran's room, where I can hear heavy snoring, and head to the kitchen for a bowl of cereal. As I eat, I think about Black Magic. I know that he was a champion at the World Yo-Yo Contest a few years ago, although I don't remember in which division. I plan to check online, and then I remember that Spader now owns

Gran's computer. I crunch down hard on the cereal, biting my tongue, which only makes me madder.

Gran is still sleeping, so after breakfast I head down the narrow hall to the living room to practice my tricks, even try a few new ones. I release two yo-yos with one hand, trying to make them both spin simultaneously. I have visions of tossing four yo-yos at once, two in each hand, impressing everyone, especially Black Magic. But my yo-yos tangle and flatline.

"Stop it," I say aloud. I know I'm going to win. So what's the problem?

I shower, gel my spikes, decide what to wear.

When the phone rings, I figure it's Van. I pick up the phone and try to sound cheerful. "How's your daughter today?"

"What? Calvin, is that you?" The gruff male voice jerks me to attention.

"Who's this?" I snap back, just like Rozelle would.

"I want to talk to Nancy Layne," he demands. "Is this the right number?"

I know who it is. I sink onto a stack of boxes. My father.

"Hello?" he yells. "What's going on?"

"Dad?" My voice wavers.

There's silence at the other end. A scuffling sound. Then, "Calvin?"

I nod, like he can see me. My throat's dry, and words won't come.

"You sound—older," he says.

"I am." Six years older than when you left, I think. Three since you last bothered to visit.

"Your grandmother there?" he finally says.

"Uh..." My tongue is thick and slow. "She's asleep." I say. Then I add, "She's sick."

"Yeah, I heard," he grunts. "Van left a message with a friend of mine."

There's that damn silence again, but the words are building up inside me, gathering into a clump, pushing to break out. "Where are you, Dad?" I sound like a whiny kid.

"West coast," he says. "South of Seattle."

"What town?"

"Can you wake her? This is long distance, and I don't know when I can call again."

"Uh, okay." What if he hangs up? Or disappears again? "Just a minute. Don't go anywhere."

"Thanks, son," he says, and something breaks off in my chest and starts to throb.

I blink back tears, set the phone on the stack of boxes and run for Gran's room.

"Gran. Wake up. Hurry." I nudge her awake and pull off the covers. "Dad's on the phone."

Her eyes widen. She looks confused, exhausted and shocked all at once, but she pulls herself up. "Get my robe," she croaks.

I snatch her robe from the chair and help her into it. My hands tremble and our eyes lock. She grips my hand briefly before we head down the hall to the living room.

I race ahead and grab the phone. "You still there?"

"'Course I am. Put her on."

Gran shuffles into the living room in her lace-trimmed pink robe, wheezing a bit. I can tell a cough's coming on.

"When are you coming home?" I say. My whole body tenses up, waiting.

Gran starts hacking, holding her chest where her robe gapes open.

"Just let me talk to her."

"But, Dad—"

"I can't do this now, Calvin." His voice has an edge that could slice me open.

I shove the phone at Gran, who's finished coughing. Her blue eyes are watery, and the skin around them is gray.

"Richard?" Her voice is rough.

I hover at her elbow, listening to Gran's side of the conversation, wishing I could hear more.

"I've been better," Gran says. "It's this cough...and there's pain in my back. The doctor's doing some tests... I've sold the shop...yes, I know...over forty years." She sighs. "Calvin is a big help, but with Van gone, it was too much to handle."

Gran asks the same questions I did. "Where are you? When are you coming home?"

She doesn't ask: *Why did you leave?* It's the question I want to ask most of all, but I'm not sure I want to hear the answer.

"What do you mean you're not coming home?" Gran says, and my heart contracts.

I strain to hear the low growl of his answer, but I can't make out the words.

"But Calvin needs you. I need you." Gran's lips tremble as she listens. "I realize that you have responsibilities. Yes...I understand. But—" She listens, pursing her lips. "At least leave your number. For heaven's sake, he's your son!"

I shut my eyes and turn away. There's more growling from the other end of the line. Then Gran whispers, "A pen! Get a pen!"

I scramble to find one among the unwashed plates, string and packing tape on the coffee table. When I stampede over to her with a stubby pencil, our fingers fumble. Then Gran grips the pencil and scribbles down a number on the flap of a cardboard box, her hand shaking so much that the figures are wobbly. "I've got it, but really, Richard, don't you think you owe the boy more than that?" She listens for a while. "Yes, I know. We all miss her. But—" She droops. "I'll tell him."

She hangs up.

"What?" I want to scream but only a whisper comes out. "Tell me what?"

Gran sighs heavily. She shuffles to the couch, lowers herself and regards me grimly. "He's not coming home." She wrinkles her forehead. "It seems he can't leave his job."

"His job?" My head feels pinched and tight. How could his job be more important than his sick mother and his only son?

"He's working on a show, designing the lights. Apparently, there's a deadline." Gran pats the couch beside her. She holds out an arm. "Come here." Her white hair is a tangled mess. Her robe and nightgown are riding up one leg, showing the large purple veins on her thigh.

I flop beside her and let her drape an arm around me.

"The job's just an excuse," Gran says. "I think...I think you remind him of your mother." She rubs my shoulder, but I can hardly feel it. "At least we have his number now. We know where he is."

I swallow. My eyes are hot and sore. He's never coming home. Why didn't I see it?

"Maybe we can..." Gran's voice fails.

When I glance at her, she's staring into space.

•••

I tell Gran we don't need my father. Then I try to forget about him by keeping busy—making food for Gran, spinning some tricks, keeping my thoughts focused on the duel.

By three o'clock, I'm more than ready to head out. I have an hour to get there and set up. I check my hair in my bedroom mirror one more time. I'm shoving my yo-yos and extra string into my backpack when Gran appears in my doorway, dressed to go out, her purse on her arm.

"Where are you going?" I ask.

"Will you come to the appointment with me?" Her eyes are cloudy. "I...I could use some help."

"What appointment?" I clench my jaw. "You never mentioned one."

"It's for"—she gives me a confused look—"a test… the doctor…" She starts rummaging through her purse. "I don't remember exactly."

"I have a show, Gran." I shift from foot to foot, eager to get going. She probably has the time or date wrong—that is, if she even has an appointment.

Gran pulls a bent appointment card from her purse. "Here it is."

<u>*Nancy Layne*</u>
has an appointment at
the Eastside Medical Clinic
<u>July 9, 4 PM</u>

"Crap," I mutter. "It's today." Could this day get any worse?

"What's that, Richard?" Gran says.

Richard. It's like a punch to the gut. "Don't call me Richard," I say a bit too loud. "I'm Calvin."

"Oh!" Gran's hand flutters to her mouth. "Did I do that? I'm so sorry. I got jumbled after that phone call…" Her eyes water.

"No, I'm sorry, Gran." I take her hand. "It's just that I have a yo-yo show, a really important one. I hate to ask this, but do you think that, if I take you there, you can get a cab home by yourself?"

Gran dries her eyes. "Okay, Richard," she says.

I sigh. Gran still has Richard, even if I've lost my father.

•••

As I'm helping Gran down the steep stairs from the apartment, Spader appears in the alley.

"Mrs. Layne," he begins, "I'm so glad to run into you."

"We can't talk now." I support Gran's elbow as she lowers herself down the final step. "We're late for an appointment at the clinic." I shoot him a look, hoping he'll feel guilty for harassing Gran.

Spader frowns, obviously frustrated. "I understand. Perhaps when you get back, Mrs. Layne? I'd like to discuss something your grandson told me—"

"We'll be gone for hours." I weave Gran around him, hoping he'll back off.

"Yes, we'll talk later." Gran nods, but I can tell she's still out of it.

I check my watch constantly on the subway, hoping I won't be late for the duel. Once Gran is safely delivered to the clinic, I run back to the station, trying not to think about her traveling home alone.

By the time I arrive at Dundas Square, I'm feeling guilty about abandoning Gran, and I'm still shaken by my father's phone call, but I try to block it all from my mind. Tall buildings with flashing billboards tower over the square. On the south side, water jets into the air through metal grates set into the stone tiles. There's a massive stage with a mike on a stand at one side and real theater lights suspended from an overhanging roof. Rozelle is on the steps leading up to the stage, doing an interview with Roberta Chow, the reporter from Urban-TV News. A cameraman is filming them while Sasha, Annette and Marshall watch. A few people slow down to check out the scene.

"We'll start with one of our yo-yo masters performin' a single-yo-yo trick, which the other has to repeat," Rozelle is saying to the reporter. "We'll see who can toss each trick the best. Then they get three minutes to freestyle. Impress the crowd."

"Who determines the winner?" the reporter asks. Her black hair falls to her shoulders, and she's got one hand on her waist.

"It's up to the crowd." Rozelle grins. "Whoever gets the most noise."

Sasha smirks as she notices me. Her bruises are either gone or covered with makeup. Marshall breaks away to head over to me, while Rozelle continues her interview.

"What do you think of the redesigned blog?" His hair is dyed black now with blue streaks, although both piercings are still there. "I think it could get nominated for a Webby Award."

"I, uh, haven't seen it yet." I make a fist, thinking of Gran's computer. "My computer...crashed." I consider explaining, but it's easier to lie.

Marshall's smile fades fast. His eyes look wounded.

"But I hear it's great," I add.

That's not enough for Marshall, I can tell. I should have found a way to check it out. An awkward silence hangs between us till he finds an excuse to escape.

I'm disappointing everyone, it seems. Rozelle slides over to me, a grin plastered on her face. "The talent ain't supposed to be late," she hisses through her smile.

"Personal emergency." I shrug. As if I owe her an explanation.

"Yeah, right." Her eyes narrow.

"You think I'm lying? I don't need—"

She grips my arm and squeezes hard. "Don't even think 'bout disrespectin' me today."

My face gets hot, and my throat tightens. Before I can think of a comeback, Rozelle is gone, the reporter is in my face and the cameraman is aiming his lens at me.

"Roberta Chow reporting for Urban-TV Community News. I'm here at Dundas Square with Yo-Yo Prophet Calvin Layne before the big face-off for the title of Local Yo-Yo Master. How do you feel about taking on Black Magic today?" She thrusts the mike closer.

"Uh, okay," I mutter, still furious at Rozelle.

"Black Magic won the World Yo-Yo Contest in the one-handed division two years in a row," she continues. "How do you plan to beat him?"

"Just, uh, throw my best." I glance around. "Is he here yet?" I vaguely remember watching his routines online, but I see no one who matches my memory of him—tall, thin, maybe twenty years old, Latino and way better-looking than me.

"He's over there." Roberta Chow nods. "Are you still predicting you'll win?"

My stomach tightens as I recognize him. Black Magic is dressed in dark leather pants and a form-fitting T-shirt that ripples over his six-pack. He's wearing fingerless gloves and leather boots, with a yo-yo holster strapped to his waist.

“Sure, I will.” I plaster on a smile.

“The Yo-Yo Prophet confirms his prediction,” Roberta Chow says to the camera. “We'll soon see how accurate he is.”

She signals the cameraman to cut the shot, and I'm hustled to center stage along with Black Magic, who's more than a two heads taller than me.

He's catching a limited-edition, top-of-the-line, gold-plated yo-yo, which I know sells for over $300. I pull out my lame neon yo-yo and slide my backpack to the side of the stage.

Rozelle saunters toward the mike, her hips swinging and her earrings jangling. As she passes, she hisses in my ear, “You better hit this, Yo-Yo.”

Hit this or I'll hit you, she means. And for once, I don't want to be in front of the crowd that's beginning to gather. I don't want to try to please them, make them throw money, predict their lives.

Maybe it's the dream, or my dad's phone call, that throws me off. Maybe it's Marshall, Rozelle, the reporter—all in my face. Maybe I'm just tired of holding myself—and Gran—together.

But the camera is catching my every movement, every twitch, and the reporter is keeping up a steady stream of commentary that I can barely hear over the noise from the crowd.

"You ready, kid?" Black Magic has that day-old stubble girls supposedly like, while I can't even grow a single facial hair. "Let's see what you got."

I manage a nod. My breath quickens. This guy has so much more experience than I do. Why did I ever predict I could win?

From the side of the stage, Annette cues a Teknonaut tune. As the music starts, my blood pumps faster. Rozelle grips the mike.

"Yo, people! Check it out!" Her voice booms across the square, making people stare. "We got two yo-yo masters dukin' it out. The Yo-Yo Prophet and Black Magic are 'bout to battle to the death." She shifts her hips and nods at us. "Kick it, boys."

Black Magic looks at me expectantly, but my hands are too jittery. "You can go first," I say, hoping I sound generous.

Black Magic winks at me and then hurls out a wicked variation of a double iron whip that could knock me flat.

The crowd hoots, and someone lets out a long whistle.

"Your turn," he says.

My throat constricts. I can't get enough air. I've never tried to throw a double iron whip, forget about his damn variation. I'm doomed.

"That was Black Magic kickin' butt!" Rozelle hoots. Whose side is she on?

Black Magic salutes the crowd, which brings more whistles and applause.

"What'd ya call that move?" Rozelle thrusts out a hip.

"The magic whip." He grins.

Rozelle smirks and then bellows to the crowd. "Who wants to see the Yo-Yo Prophet crack a magic whip?"

A weak cheer leaves me feeling more than useless.

"This here's a duel for real, folks." Rozelle tosses her hair, which she's straightened to hang to her shoulders. "The Yo-Yo Prophet has gotta repeat the trick, or lose a life!"

Maybe she's trying to rev up the crowd. Maybe she wants him to win. Either way, I'm frozen in place, staring out at the audience.

Faces zoom in and out of focus. Joseph seems to be moving his mouth in slow motion, and I hear the slurry words, "Go, Yo-Yo!" Eleanor Rizzo is clapping. Marshall is scribbling in his notebook, probably about how crappy I am. I recognize Geordie—I can't believe he came. My eyes leap over Sasha. I can't take her venom right now.

How do I get out of this?

Then I see the gray-eyed girl near the front. She's waving up at me and looking awesome in a silver top that makes her eyes glimmer. I shake my head, clearing a mess of thoughts.

I predicted she would come. And she did.

I predicted I would beat Black Magic. And I will.

My breathing slows. Time speeds up. Sound rushes back in. I hear Rozelle going on about dueling to the death. The crowd is getting worked up, probably eager for blood. What am I afraid of? I'm the Yo-Yo Prophet.

I pitch out my yo-yo, hoping for the best. I struggle through a jade whip, which is less advanced but the most I can do. No one but Black Magic and I know the tricks, so what does it matter?

Except that the camera is recording my moves. And there may be other yo-yo fanatics watching.

The crowd claps a bit. I try to breathe. The sun beats down, making me sweat. The giant billboards flash. The music's techno beat hammers at me relentlessly.

"The Yo-Yo Prophet cracks it!" Rozelle bellows across the square. "Let's see you bust another move!" She winks at me.

The cameraman zooms in. Joseph is cheering louder than anyone. I gulp in some air and perform his favorite trick.

"Buddha's revenge," I say. It's a solid effort.

The crowd applauds. I feel lighter, higher.

Black Magic matches the trick—no problem. With his tight leather pants and long black hair, he looks so damn cool, like he has nothing to prove.

We're even now, with two tricks each, when Black Magic throws out a Yuuki slack. It's a trick first performed by Yuuki Spencer at the World Yo-Yo Contest. When he threw it, the audience went wild.

So does this crowd.

It's a master-level move. Although I've tried it before, I've never done it successfully. I straighten my shoulders and go for it anyway.

"Yuuki slack." I nod to Black Magic, Rozelle, the crowd, like I'm facing a firing squad. I launch into the trick. It starts with a trapeze and moves into a double or nothing. The secret is to pinch the string while it's looping, slackening it and then whipping the loop back and forth between your hands while rotating the yo-yo.

I bomb, sending the yo-yo into a spin-out.

"Shit," I mutter.

The crowd doesn't boo me off the stage, but they don't cheer much either.

"Ouch!" Rozelle struts the stage. "That's one for Black Magic. The Yo-Yo Prophet better pull up!" She shoots me a warning glance. Maybe she is rooting for me after all. I guess she wouldn't want me to fail. Or would she?

The torture continues with three more tricks, which I barely manage. It's obvious to everyone that Black Magic is a pro, and I'm not.

When the crowd has built up to about a hundred people, Rozelle announces that round one goes to Black Magic, although I can make it back in round two. Freestyle.

I'm doing my best to ignore the reporter and the camera as Rozelle tells the crowd, "Each of these boys gets three minutes to showcase their best. All you gotta do is cheer for your favorite."

"You first." I nod to Black Magic, figuring I better see what he's got so I can try to outdo him.

Black Magic conjures a slew of master-level tricks that rage against me. Double suicide. Reverse trapeze whip. Kamikaze. Superman. Tricks I can't even follow with my eyes.

He starts into a ladder escape, popping the yo-yo in and out of a triangle formation in the string so fast that gold sparks seem to shoot from his yo-yo.

It's an awesome routine—he's even invented new tricks. It casts a spell over the screeching mob.

"Time!" Rozelle shouts. In my daze, I realize that she's been using a stopwatch.

I'm trembling, waiting for her to call the start of my lousy routine, but the crowd won't stop chanting Black Magic's name.

That's when I see the gray-eyed girl, staring dreamily up at him.

I turn away.

Forget her, I think.

"Yeah, folks! Now that's a cheer." Rozelle throws me a concerned look. "But wait till you see our own Yo-Yo Prophet!"

The crowd screams and yells for Black Magic.

I am so dead.

Rozelle raises one arm to start the countdown. Her bicep quivers. I snap to attention, fingers tingling, every muscle tense.

"Now." She lowers her arm.

I throw out my yo-yo like a life preserver into the ocean and then dive in after it.

No thoughts, just my hands working the string, the yo-yo flying. I'm throwing strong; my sleepers last forever. I do a shockwave. Cold fusion. Laceration.

I'm in the zone. I can do this, I think. I can beat this sucker.

That's my prediction. It has to happen. I have to make it happen.

I move into the beginning of my most ambitious sequence of tricks. My grand finale will stun the crowd, make them scream only for me. I shoot my yo-yo skyward, soaring above the crashing ocean waves. My yo-yo extends gloriously on the string. It grips, ready to reverse direction. Then my string breaks.

"No-o-o-o!" I yell.

Time slows down. The string jerks in a crazy snake-like dance. My yo-yo arcs high over the crowd, heading for the jets of water that spurt from the ground into the square.

I fumble for my backpack—my extra yo-yos.

"I can start again," I plead.

There's a free-for-all as a few people scramble toward my wayward yo-yo like it's some kind of trophy.

The crowd starts chanting Black Magic's name. Rozelle is shooting daggers my way.

"It's just a broken string," I say.

The crowd won't shut up. They keep cheering, "Ma-gic! Ma-gic!" It goes on and on. No one cares that I've pulled another yo-yo from my pack. No one wants me to try again.

Rozelle fires me a desperate look. She hollers, "The winner is…Black Magic!" Her eyebrows knot.

My shoulders slump. The crowd roars even louder.

The reporter leaps onto the stage—a hunter closing in on her kill. She's got her mike ready, questions already forming on her lips. She positions herself next to me as the cameraman follows her up. Rozelle stomps over to Black Magic and congratulates him, although she's red-faced and glowering.

"How do you feel about your first failed prediction?" The reporter drives the mike into my face. The cameraman has me in his sights.

"I guess I'm not one-hundred-percent accurate all the time." I shrink away.

The reporter nods and swivels to Black Magic. "It looks like you crushed your competition. Are you surprised by today's events?"

Black Magic shrugs. "Strings break. It doesn't mean I won. The kid is pretty good."

The crowd doesn't agree. They yell his name, ask for more. The gray-eyed girl calls up to him, "You smashed that routine." She lifts her silky blond hair off her neck and lets it fall in a slow cascade.

Black Magic ignores her. He slips his yo-yo into his holster. "Tough luck, kid," he says to me before he saunters away.

The music ends abruptly; the crowd is thinning. I try to slide away too, crawl into a crack in the granite slabs of the square, but Sasha is suddenly onstage, blocking my escape.

"This isn't the first prophecy he's gotten wrong," she says loud enough for the reporter to hear. "The whole thing's a joke. He's a joke." She glares down at me through mascara-laden eyelashes.

I grind my teeth. This day is bad enough without Sasha getting in my face. "What's your problem?" I say to her, not caring who hears. "Why are you always out to get me?"

"Because I'm sick of covering your ass," she hisses and turns to the reporter. "He can throw a yo-yo"—

she smirks—"most of the time, but everything he predicts..." She gestures toward Annette over by the speakers. "We have to make it happen."

"What are you talking about?" I glance at Rozelle, whose jaw is clenched as she glares at Sasha. My palms are sweaty. What has Rozelle done this time?

The reporter perks up. She positions her damn mike in Sasha's stupid face. "Are you calling Calvin Layne a false prophet?"

People in the crowd are listening—Eleanor Rizzo, Marshall, Joseph, Geordie—now that Black Magic has left the stage.

"Yup." Sasha flips her bangs off her face. "The first time he made a prediction, we had to help this woman"—she points to Eleanor Rizzo—"get a job. Which wasn't too hard, since my uncle owns a copy shop downtown."

Eleanor Rizzo gasps.

Rozelle says, "Don't lie, Sasha."

"Give it up, Roz." Sasha juts out her chin.

"Let me clarify. The Yo-Yo Prophet predicted she'd get that job?" the reporter asks. "But you made sure it happened?"

Sasha nods at the camera. "Ever since then, we've had to run around and make sure his predictions came true."

I shut my eyes briefly. This can't be happening.

"When he said some man would find his lost cat, we had to search for it. When he told this guy he would pass his science exam, we had to pay for a tutor. We even broke up this woman and her boyfriend by flirting with him. Whatever he said, we had to make it happen." She snorts.

"Is he ever right?" the reporter asks.

Sasha shrugs. "Sometimes, but it's just a fluke."

"So you lied to the media about your predictions?" Marshall is pale and furious. His pen is poised above his notebook, ready to record my every word.

"I...I didn't know...," I say, even though part of me did. I knew Rozelle was making me into a liar, a cheat, a fool. I just didn't want to admit it.

Even Geordie is shaking his head. I guess he doesn't think much of me now.

"Don't listen to her." Rozelle's neck muscles are tight cords. "She's just jealous. Right, Annette?"

Annette backs away, almost tripping over a speaker wire.

My stomach clenches and unclenches like a fist. If only I'd never met Rozelle. If only I'd never listened to her. She did this to me.

"This is your fault," I say to her.

"Watch what you say, Yo-Yo." Rozelle's voice is threatening.

"Just leave me alone." I grab my backpack, jump off the stage and race across the square. I take the stairs down to the subway two at a time, fleeing the judgmental faces, the reporter's questions, the camera lens capturing my humiliation for the world to see.

The train takes forever to arrive. I keep my head down, too embarrassed to look anyone in the eye. How long until my shame is out there for everyone to see? On TV? On my blog? Or Marshall's?

When the train finally squeals into the station, I slink into a seat in the last car. How could I have been so stupid? I knew Rozelle couldn't be trusted.

I just want to go home—stay there forever.

Half an hour later, I'm slipping into the alley behind the store, inhaling the stench from the Dumpster. The sun is low in the sky, making long shadows against the buildings.

Luckily, I avoid Spader. When I get to the metal staircase leading to our apartment, a pale white arm dangles over the top step. Someone's collapsed on the landing.

"Gran!" I race up the stairs, stumbling, desperate.

The door is half open. Gran's key is in the lock. And Gran is lying at an awkward angle, eyes closed, her head jammed sideways against the railing.

I kneel beside Gran and fold her dangling arm over her stomach, watch her chest for signs of breathing.

"Gran! Talk to me!" My voice cracks.

The metal grid of the landing digs into my knees. The setting sun shines on Gran's face. I nudge her, pat her cheek. Anything to make her wake up.

A lifetime passes. Gran coughs. Her eyes flutter open.

"Richard?" she croaks.

"I'm here." I deserve to be called Richard. I abandoned her too.

She tries to adjust her twisted neck. "It hurts," she moans.

“Don’t move, Gran.” I remember that from health class. “I’m going to get help.”

I glance down at the alley, but there’s no one in sight.

“Wait here,” I say, and then realize how dumb I sound.

I step over Gran and push open the door to the apartment. The hall is dark. I dump my backpack, race for the phone, call 9-1-1.

When a woman answers, I scream into the mouthpiece: “I need an ambulance! It’s my grandmother. Please, hurry!” It’s all I can do to remember our address.

•••

The ambulance ride is a blur. I huddle in a corner, out of the way, while the medic hovers over Gran. He’s wearing a black uniform with *EMS* on the shoulder. His partner is driving. They’ve trapped Gran in a neck collar and carrying-board with straps. She has an oxygen mask over her nose and mouth.

“It’s my fault,” I tell the medic.

He’s adjusting the IV tube that runs into her hand. “You didn’t do this to her,” the medic says.

“I left her alone.”

“And you called nine-one-one.”

The siren wails, and the driver answers the crackling radio.

What if it's too late? I want to ask, but I can't say the words.

Gran coughs till tears stream down her face.

I can't watch. I stare at the white ceiling, letting the ambulance rock me as we round the corner.

At the hospital, they move Gran onto a bed and draw the curtain around her. I'm allowed to sit in a chair beside her bed. I hug my knees, answer the nurses' questions, watch them wheel her away for tests, watch them wheel her back.

"Is there an adult we can call?" the admitting nurse asks. "Your parents? An aunt?"

As if my father would come.

"My dad's out of town," I say, which isn't exactly a lie. "My mom's dead."

When she mentions Family Services, I quickly backtrack, saying that I've got family friends to help me out. She suggests I call my father right away. Like he would come.

It's a long night.

The hospital reminds me of when my mother was sick: It smells like hand sanitizer and death. Doctors and nurses hustle up and down the hallways. Strange machines beep warning signals. The fluorescent lights in the halls never dim.

My mother lost her hair. Her eyes sank into her skull. Her lips cracked. One day, she didn't wake up.

I rock back and forth in the chair. "Don't leave me, Gran," I whisper.

If only I had stayed with her. If only I had missed the duel. If only the camera hadn't recorded it all.

I'm an idiot, I think. And now everyone knows it.

I lean my head against the chair.

I don't fall asleep till morning.

•••

Gran is still snoring when I wake up.

My neck is cramped. My legs are sore. I stretch against the hospital chair, listening to Gran's gurgling breaths and trying to forget the nightmare that was yesterday. Why did I let Rozelle control me? I acted like a fool when I should have been watching out for Gran.

When Gran lets out a long wheeze, I reach through the sidebars on her bed.

The neck brace and straps are gone, although tubes still weave into her nose and arm. Her skin is paler than ever. Her cheeks are gray.

"I'm sorry, Gran." I grip her fingers.

She moans in her sleep.

After a while, a red-haired nurse in a mint-green uniform enters. She checks Gran's pulse, temperature and blood pressure. Gran hardly stirs.

I sit up straight. "What's wrong with her?" They've asked me a million questions about Gran's health. Now, I want some answers.

"The doctor will talk to you soon." She gives me a sympathetic smile. "Why don't you get some food? There's a cafeteria on the fourth floor."

I shake my head. "I can't leave her." I don't have my backpack anyway, which means I have no money. I must have left it in the apartment.

The day passes slowly. Gran wakes briefly a few times, but she doesn't say much.

"I don't think so, Your Majesty," she mumbles once.

I drink water from the bathroom and nibble the food they bring for Gran.

Near the end of the day, the red-haired nurse catches me eating Gran's Jell-O.

"Why don't you go home for some food and a rest? Maybe get your grandmother a few things? She'll need a toothbrush, a nightgown, slippers."

I never thought of that. "Yeah, I guess that would be a good idea."

Then she asks, "Is your father here yet?"

How does she know about him? I tense up. "Not yet."

"Well, I hope you have someone at home. A friend? Neighbor?"

I think of Van on the other side of the country, of Lucy's casseroles, of Franco's concerned eyes. "I have a lot of help." I try to sound confident. "Family friends, you know? Lucy makes a different casserole every day."

"Good. So someone's staying with you until your father gets home?"

Wow, she knows too much. "I'm fine—except for the macaroni casserole." I shrug. "I could do without that."

I leave the hospital, if only to get away from the nurse's questions. I don't need to be reminded that Gran is the only family I have left.

On my way through the alley to the apartment, I see Van's old chair sticking out of the Dumpster. She used to sit out back when she took a break. She didn't seem to mind the stench of garbage, or the slick layer of grease on the asphalt. She'd just sit on that worn-out kitchen chair and smile at the sparrows hopping along the crooked cedar fence separating the alley from the row of backyards. Once, I saw her feeding her lunch to a stray cat.

I consider yanking Van's chair free of the bin—setting it against the brick wall where it belongs—but it won't make any difference. Spader will just toss it out again. And I need to get back to Gran.

I climb the stairs to the apartment, planning what I'll pack for her. When I get to the landing, I cringe, remembering how I found her lying there.

I pull myself together and head inside. In the kitchen, I find a note from Lucy explaining how to heat the meatloaf she left in the fridge—I guess Gran gave her a key. I rummage through Gran's closet, shoving some clothes into my backpack, along with a little money from my stash. My twin racers are still in one of the pockets, but I don't touch them. They've brought me enough trouble. I don't even miss my neon yo-yo.

I'm starting to stink, so I quickly shower and change my clothes. As I cram some cold meatloaf into my mouth, I consider phoning Van for help, but I don't want to tell her how badly I've messed up. What would she do anyway? She's with her own family now.

I sling my backpack over one shoulder, ready to go. At the last minute, I give in to a sudden urge to call my dad's number. It rings forever and then goes to voicemail.

I hang up without leaving a message.

My skin feels raw, like someone has peeled back a few layers, leaving me exposed and blistered.

The rain batters the hospital window and runs down the glass. Through the rippling water, I stare out at the night. Car headlights flash and then streak away. Thunder growls across the starless sky. Streetlights reflect in the puddles.

I panicked when I returned to the hospital and found Gran's bed empty. I started blubbering at the nurses' station, wailing like a freak.

It turns out that Gran has been moved to a different room. The doctor had come—while I was gone—and told her she had to stay for a few days.

I'm sure all the nurses are talking about my meltdown. Or maybe they're used to it. Either way, I don't have to face those nurses again. On this new ward, I've seen a

Jamaican nurse who's too busy to talk and a grumpy gray-haired one I plan to avoid.

Gran coughs in her sleep and rolls on her side. I'm jammed in a chair between her bed and the window in the darkened room, trying to stay off the nurses' radar, using yet another hospital chair for a bed. This one has low arms, which I can't lean against, and a straight back. I wish it reclined. The other bed in this room is empty, but I don't dare use it.

It's only about eleven o'clock, but I'm sure I'll never get to sleep. My mind churns like Gran's old computer trying to download a large video file. I think about Gran's illness getting worse, our failed search for a new apartment, Rozelle bossing me around. I had everything under control before I crashed and burned at the duel. Or did I? All the signs were there. I just refused to see them.

I shiver as the air-conditioning cycles on.

One good thing about the hospital: No one knows we're here. It's like we've escaped for a while, although it won't be for long enough.

I sigh and cross my legs, trying to get comfortable.

Gran's heavy breathing fills the room. I worry that she's sleeping too much. Maybe it's the drugs they're giving her. Maybe it's something worse.

I shut my eyes and try to force sleep to come.

•••

I wake to someone shaking me.

The room is dark, except for the blinding rectangle of light from the hall door.

"Gran?" I mumble. "Is it time for school?"

"Who you calling Gran?" snaps a female voice with a thick Jamaican accent. "Wake yourself up and get on home! This isn't a hotel."

I jump to my feet, head reeling. Gran is sleeping in a hospital bed. The horror rushes back in.

"How'd you get in here anyway?" The nurse has her hands on her hips.

"That's my grandmother," I plead. "I have to stay with her."

"It's four in the morning!" she says, although her expression softens. "Come back during visiting hours."

"But they let me stay last night—"

"Not on my floor." She nudges me toward the hall. "I've got enough people to watch. I don't need you hanging around."

The nurse blocks my view of Gran, although I can hear her snoring as loud as ever. I grab my backpack and scurry out of the room, squinting at the fluorescent lights in the hall.

"Make sure you take care of her." I glance back. Then I head down to the emergency department, where the waiting room is packed with dozing people.

I'm sure one more won't hurt.

•••

I spend the rest of the night avoiding the hospital security guards. In the morning, I get my breakfast from the vending machine—three packages of chocolate-chip cookies—and sneak past the new shift of nurses to Gran's room. I find Gran awake, staring into space, too doped up to know what's going on. When a woman in a white lab coat bustles in, I'm licking chocolate off my fingers, although my stomach is growling for more.

"Oh!" The woman startles when she sees me.

I leap up, scattering wrappers on the floor. "Are you her doctor?"

"Yes, I'm Dr. Chen." She shoves her hands in the pockets of her lab coat and frowns slightly. "Are you a relative?"

"I'm her grandson, Calvin Layne," I say. The inside of my mouth feels like it's coated in slime. I wish I'd brought my toothbrush.

"Visiting hours start in"—she glances at the wall clock—"three hours."

"I know. Please don't kick me out. I need to be with her." I stand tall, trying to look as mature as possible, like I won't cause any trouble.

Dr. Chen regards me skeptically, although her eyes are kind. "Where's the rest of your family?"

"Uh, my dad's out getting breakfast." It could be true, and I sure don't want Family Services to get involved. "Can I stay?"

"I suppose for now you're not bothering anyone." She glances at the empty bed beside Gran's. "But next time, follow the rules." She moves to Gran's bedside.

"Great. Thanks." I pick my wrappers off the floor and dump them in the garbage. I watch Dr. Chen, hoping she'll tell me what's wrong with Gran.

Dr. Chen brushes a strand of hair off Gran's face. "How are you today, Nancy?"

"Fine, Your Majesty," Gran slurs, waving her away.

I cringe and step closer, so I'm on the opposite side of the bed from Dr. Chen.

The doctor glances at me. "Your grandson's here early. He seems very fond of you."

"Calvin is a good boy." Gran smiles in my general direction, and I reach for her hand. I'm glad she remembers my name, although I'm not sure how good I am.

"His father stepped out to get breakfast. Did you see him earlier?"

My eyes get wide. Is Dr. Chen checking up on me?

"Richard's not here right now," Gran mumbles.

For the first time ever, I'm glad Gran is not alert.

Dr. Chen nods. "I understand you run a dry-cleaning business?"

"For more than forty years." Gran sighs. Her eyelids droop and her grip on my hand relaxes.

"She sold it though," I say. "We're moving soon."

"Good." Dr. Chen nods again and says to Gran, "I suspect that your health issues may be a result of prolonged exposure to perc. Did you use it in your cleaning process?"

Gran nods, and then her eyes shut, like she can't keep them open any longer.

"In that case, I'd like to identify the specific chemicals involved. Is that possible? Nancy?"

Gran struggles to open her eyes and fails.

"Maybe we should talk about this later," Dr. Chen says.

"What's perc?" I ask. I never paid much attention to the cleaning process. I only worked the front counter.

"It's short for perchloroethylene—a chemical used in dry cleaning. It can cause dizziness, confusion, inflammation of the respiratory system, fluid build-up in the lungs, kidney problems—all of which your grandmother has."

"Is she going to get better?"

"Of course I am," Gran mutters, her eyes still closed.

Dr. Chen and I exchange smiles.

"I agree, Nancy. Your symptoms should improve now that you're away from the perc. Although there is a danger that, over long periods of time, perc can cause more permanent problems..." Her voice trails off.

"Like what?" I'm instantly on edge.

Dr. Chen glances at me and then looks away.

"Please," I whisper. "We have to know."

Gran mumbles, but I can't make out what she saying.

"Maybe we should discuss worst-case scenarios when your dad gets here," Dr. Chen says. "I've reduced your grandmother's pain medication, so she'll become more alert shortly. We can talk then."

"It's bad, isn't it?" I think of my mother. "Just tell me it's not cancer," I beg.

Dr. Chen's eyes remain steady, but her forehead furrows.

I swallow hard.

"We need to think positively." Dr. Chen examines my face, as if she really cares how I feel. "We should know more soon. In the meantime, I promise I'll do everything I can. Okay?"

I nod, unable to speak.

Dr. Chen checks the clock and gives me a sympathetic smile. "It's still a while until visiting hours start, but you can stay with your grandmother, as long as you're quiet. I'll let the nurses know you're here."

"Thanks." My hands are jittery. I reach into my pocket for a yo-yo, but there's nothing there.

• • •

Although I'm afraid to leave Gran for long, my stomach eventually demands more food. At lunch time, I head to the cafeteria, where I buy some pizza. There's a TV tuned to the local news.

I eat my pizza quickly, eyes on the screen. It's not Urban-TV News, but it gets me thinking. Did they air the duel? Is it posted on YouTube? Am I a laughingstock yet? I don't want to see the video, but I can't stop myself. I have to find out how bad it is.

I hurry down the street to the public library. Inside, there are two rows of computer terminals with Internet access. Three people are already lined up for the computers, and I fidget while I'm waiting, thinking about Gran.

When I finally get a turn, I navigate to the Yo-Yo Prophet blog first, wondering if Marshall has taken down the site, but it's still there.

My stomach sinks when I read the title of his latest post: *Yo-Yo Prophet or Yo-Yo Profit?*

At a duel to determine the ultimate Local Yo-Yo Master, the Yo-Yo Prophet proved to be seriously outclassed by World Yo-Yo Champion Black Magic—in more ways than one.

First, Black Magic demonstrated superior yo-yo skill in trick after trick, and the crowd crowned him the clear winner of the contest.

Then Sasha Reynolds, a source close to the Yo-Yo Prophet, revealed he was a fake who relied on others to make his "predictions" come true.

The Yo-Yo Prophet? More like the Yo-Yo Profit.

We've been duped, readers. All of us. We believed the words of a cheat who tricked people out of their money with sensational lies.

I've resigned my job as personal online reporter to the Yo-Yo Profit and revised his prediction accuracy rate on this site. Take a look at the stats. This guy is clearly a fake.

I grind my teeth. Like it was ever about the money. Marshall doesn't get it. And he doesn't even mention Rozelle. Like it's all my fault. Although maybe it is. I'm the fool who followed her.

I scroll through a few of the blog comments, which read more like hate mail.

As soon as I saw him, I knew this kid was a flake…

…just another scam artist preying on innocent people…

I want to leave my own comment, but what would I say? You're right? I *am* a loser?

Marshall estimated my prediction accuracy rate to be forty percent. Some record.

I think back to the last predictions I made about my own life: Gran is worse, not better. We still haven't found a new apartment. The gray-eyed girl isn't interested in me. And I'm no yo-yo master. A zero-percent accuracy rate. Nice.

I can hardly bear to watch the newscast on YouTube. Black Magic looks like a god beside me. The reporter smiles as if she's enjoying my failure. I hate Rozelle for making me look stupid. I hate how everyone can see my humiliation forever. I hate that reporter for ever taking an interest in me.

I was better off when I was anonymous.

•••

For the next few days, I spend as much time at the hospital as I can, only going home when I have to.

One afternoon during visiting hours, Gran moans and struggles to sit up.

I jump to her side. "Careful." I push the button to raise the head of the bed.

"Calvin?" Gran glances around the hospital room like she's just figuring out where she is.

"How are you feeling?" I'm glad she recognizes me.

"I've been better." She grimaces, coughs and then wipes her eyes with a trembling hand. "What happened? How did I get here?"

"You fell, Gran." I sit on the edge of her bed. "When I was out." I remember her collapsed on the landing. "I'm so sorry. If only I had—"

"Oh, Calvin," Gran scolds, her voice hoarse, although she speaks without slurring. "You're my grandson, not my babysitter."

I crack half a smile. "Now I know you're feeling better." I tell her what Dr. Chen said, although I don't mention the cancer part. I'll leave that to the doctor, mostly because I can't bring myself to say the word. "You've been here for days," I finish.

Gran rests her head against the pillow. Her brow furrows. The hollows in her cheeks deepen. She's silent for a while, and then her eyes close. Just when I wonder if she's falling asleep, she says, "How was your yo-yo show?"

"Terrible," I say, surprised she remembers. I explain what happened. "I'm so stupid. I wish I could erase the video from the Internet."

Gran's face contorts with pain. She clutches the blanket.

"I'll get the nurse." I leap to my feet. My problems are nothing compared to Gran's.

"No," she croaks. "It'll pass."

I sit beside her, uneasy.

Her blue eyes are unfocused. The veins in her hands bulge beneath her pale skin. "Her Majesty knows we've both made mistakes," she mutters.

Not again. I wince. "Gran, what are you talking about?"

"Queen Elizabeth the Second." Her nose whistles as she exhales. "She's reigned for so long and so well through so many changes." She gets a faraway look. "I always wanted to be queen, ever since I was a little girl. Although I was a queen, in a way. Queen of my shop."

"I know you were," I say.

"It wasn't much, but it was mine to reign over, no matter what." She sighs. "Now I'm only queen of myself. But that's enough." She lifts her head and shoulders off the pillow, her neck muscles straining. "No illness is going to reign over me."

I hope not. I shut my eyes briefly and try not to think about Gran with cancer. "That's a good attitude." I try to sound positive.

"Of course it is." She collapses back against the pillows, obviously exhausted. "We can't control the world, but we can reign over our own little piece of it." She grips my hand. "Maybe you're not a prophet," she pauses, "but you are good with a yo-yo."

A royal lecture. I make a face and pull my hand away. "Not as good as Black Magic." Why did I ever think I could beat a world champion? I must have been seriously delusional.

"So what?" Her eyes flutter closed. "You're good enough to put on a show that people want to watch."

"Maybe." If Rozelle hadn't ruined it for me.

Then Gran mumbles, "Did you talk to Richard yet? Or Van? You shouldn't be staying alone."

"I...uh...Lucy and Franco are helping," I say. "You just take care of yourself."

I spend the rest of the afternoon watching over Gran. I'm too wired to sleep. Too tired to think straight. My gut is grumbling, but it's not hunger. More like a festering ache.

Gran kicks me out when visiting hours end.

"I'll be fine." Her eyes are crusty with sleep. "Go home. Get some rest."

On the subway, I frown out the window at the tunnel walls. My eyelids are heavy, but my mind can't stop churning.

I feel like I'm a yo-yo, getting tossed by some master player. Sometimes it's Rozelle holding the string. Sometimes Spader, my dad or even Gran. But it's rarely me. And I'm sick of it.

My hands clench. The businesswoman in the seat across from me is staring over the top of her newspaper like I'm one of those crazies who talk to themselves.

I make a get-lost face at her and duck my head for the rest of the ride. I almost miss my stop, lunging off the train just as the doors are closing. I take the escalator to street level and trudge along the sidewalk toward home.

When I pass the bank where I earned my first coins with my yo-yo, I think about the busker festival. Would I even want to face a crowd again? Would they boo me? I don't think I could stand it.

I cut into the alley when I'm a block from home. It's not dark yet. The muggy air makes it feel hotter than it is. I wipe the sweat off my forehead with my shirt. The stench from the Dumpsters turns my stomach.

As I near the stairs to our apartment, I notice the back door to the dry cleaner's is open. Hot, perfume-free air rushes out.

"No perc there," I grumble. Why is Spader so annoyingly right?

I swing one foot onto the stairs, hoping to avoid Spader. He'll only ask questions that I can't answer.

"Calvin."

Busted.

I slowly turn. Spader leans against the doorjamb and crosses his arms.

"What do you want?" I mutter.

The triangle of stubble on his chin twitches. He raises one eyebrow. "I want to know how your grandmother is—and whether she's found a new place to live. It's almost the end of the month."

"You don't need to tell me that." I'm not in the mood to deal with him.

Spader frowns. "I'm just trying to help, Calvin."

"Help?" My backpack slides down one arm, and I jerk it back up. "Yeah, you've been a lot of help."

He pinches his lips together. "How is your grandmother? I've been hoping to chat with her, but I haven't seen her recently."

Ask her doctor, I want to snap at him, but I don't want to bring Gran into it. "She's at East General Hospital… she's been there for days."

"The hospital?" Again, he jacks his eyebrow. "Is she all right?"

I shrug. Of course she isn't, but I'm not discussing it with Spader. I pivot on the stairs and start to haul myself up.

"I'm sorry to hear about your grandmother, Calvin. Is there anything I can do to help?"

"We're fine," I say without slowing my pace up the stairs.

"At least take my phone number," he insists. "In case you think of something."

"Just leave it in the mailbox," I say.

"Are you sure I can't help?" he pleads, like he's feeling guilty.

I should try to be nice, but I'm tired of him pulling my string.

"You could find us a house," I grunt. "With a garden for Gran." I reach the landing, unlock the door and open it.

"Calvin, be reasonable. I'm trying to—"

I slam the door on his words, grateful for the slab of wood between us.

•••

My footsteps echo off the walls and floor. The apartment is sweltering. I open all the windows, but it doesn't help. I shower and eat, but sleeping is impossible.

I call Van at her daughter's place. When I tell her about Gran's condition, she freaks. "So sorry," she says in Vietnamese. "I will come when I can, Calvin." Then she tells me that the baby could be born any day. "Please understand," she begs. "I am needed here too."

Next I dial my father's number. I hold my breath, waiting for him to pick up, not exactly sure what I'll say.

But I don't have to worry, because it goes to voicemail again. He's avoiding me. I stumble through a message about Gran being admitted to East General. I don't ask if he's coming home.

When I hang up, the silence closes in.

I try the TV, but there are only a few fuzzy channels since Gran canceled the cable. Normally, I'd practice new yo-yo tricks to distract myself, but just thinking about yo-yoing brings the whole mess with Rozelle crashing around me again. If only she hadn't invented the Yo-Yo Prophet, forced it down my throat. Maybe I would have seen that Gran was getting sicker. Maybe I would have realized that I wasn't a yo-yo master, just a geek who knows a few tricks.

I decide to pack the rest of the apartment, even though we have no place to go. It's better than obsessing over ways to destroy Rozelle.

I pack most of the dishes and all of Gran's clothes. After midnight, I collapse into bed and fall into a restless, dreamless sleep.

I wake early in the morning, sweating and exhausted. After another cool shower, I start packing my room. I get stalled when I get to my yo-yo collection.

I keep it in my top drawer at the front. My yo-yos are lined up in a row from oldest to newest, with my extra strings and spare parts on the left. I reach out, hesitate, run my fingers over the row. Do I dare?

I pick up one of my twin racers and slide the string over my middle finger. I haven't tossed a yo-yo since my defeat five whole days ago. I wonder if I can still pitch a simple power throw.

I launch the yo-yo, and it spins and returns to my hand like it's glad to be home. I smile. God, I love yo-yoing. The string cutting into my finger. The soft whirring sound. Even the plastic smell.

How did I screw up the Yuuki slack trick? Maybe it was the way I pinched the string. Not firmly enough. I hustle into the living room, where there's empty space between the piles of boxes and jumbled furniture. I let the yo-yo fly free into the start of a Yuuki slack…and tangle the string.

I fix the string and spin the yo-yo out once more. When the yo-yo flatlines, I toss it again. When I whack it against a stack of boxes, I check it for cracks and then go at it some more.

I toss steadily, mess up, repeat—until my finger gets raw from the string.

I collapse against the living-room wall. I slide to the floor and rip my yo-yo off.

"Forget it," I mutter. I'll never be like Black Magic.

Outside the window, dull gray clouds are gathering. I rub my finger, replaying in my mind the moment when the string broke. The vibrating string pulled taut, the horrible snap and the weightlessness as the yo-yo soared away.

It's a simple thing—a broken string. A random, destructive event. Like cancer. Only maybe that's not so random. Did Mom get cancer from perc? Will Gran?

And suddenly I'm furious at how helpless I am. I need to get a grip, take control of my piece of the world, like Gran said. Starting with my dad. Why does he get to run away? How am I supposed to handle this mess by myself?

I reach for the phone, pulling it toward me across the floor by the cord. I dial his number; I've got it memorized already. I bite my lip, waiting for him to answer, but of course, it goes to voicemail. My hand tightens around the phone. I listen to his message. My words burst out after the beep.

"Yeah, Dad, it's your son. Remember me? Just one question: Why'd you leave? I figure you ran away from what you couldn't handle. So I wonder, Dad, did it help? 'Cause right now Gran is at the hospital getting tested for cancer while I'm packing the apartment we have to leave in two weeks, even though we have no place to go." Blood throbs in my temples. "Nothing's going right.

And I can't fix any of it. You know why, Dad?" I grind out the words. "Because shit happens. We don't get to decide how things work out."

I slam the phone down. My eyes rake the empty room, looking for someone, something, to latch on to.

My twin racer lies beside me on the floor.

I pick it up. I run my thumb over it. I grip it in my fist.

Rozelle ruined yo-yoing for me. Until I met her, it was the best thing in my life.

She shouldn't get away with that.

I curse her under my breath, but it's not enough. I want to scream at her, rage till she begs for mercy, tell her what a bitch she's been.

So what's stopping me?

I dig the telephone book out of a cardboard box, remembering when Sasha once mentioned Rozelle's street. I rifle through the pages for Rozelle's address. Twelve Glebe Road. I write it on the back of a drug-store receipt. Then I hike over to Rozelle's place, before I lose my nerve.

It's midmorning when I arrive, still fuming about all the shit Rozelle has put me through. Rozelle's place is a small bungalow on a tree-lined street. There are a few flowers planted out front and a huge maple tree in the yard. Twelve Glebe Road is nicer than I expected, which pisses me off even more. Why does Rozelle talk ghetto when she comes from a place like this? It's like everything is an act to her—a game for her amusement.

She's not going to screw with me anymore. I march up the walk and knock on the edge of the screen door. The inside wooden door is open. Through the screen, familiar techno music throbs.

No one comes.

I hammer harder, peering inside, where I can see a leather couch and a large flat-screen TV. Why does Rozelle have it so good? Eventually, a silhouetted figure lumbers down the hall toward me. By the shape, I know it's Rozelle.

I tense up.

Rozelle pushes the door open with one hand. She's wearing baggy sweatpants, a tight T-shirt and no makeup. Without the heavy black eyeliner, she's not so intimidating.

"Calvin Layne." She rolls her eyes. "If you're here to give me shit, don't bother."

"I'll give you shit if I want to." It feels good to blast her. "You deserve it."

"Whatever." She starts to pull the screen door shut.

I block it with my leg. "You ruined my show!"

"You're such a lame ass." Her lip curls in disgust. "You think I did wrong by you?" She puts one hand on her hip. "I got you up onstage and made you a star. They loved the Yo-Yo Prophet—and so did you!"

"Well, they don't anymore. Did you see Marshall's last post?"

"Sure." She gives me a face full of attitude. "And did you read the comments?"

"I read enough." I snort.

She shrugs. "Nothin' like a scandal to get people hot."

"Are you crazy?"

"You got hundreds of comments on that site. People can't stop talkin' 'bout you."

"So?" I shift my weight from one foot to the other. "What good is that if they hate me?"

"You wanna be loved, or do you wanna have a kick-ass audience at your next gig?"

"What gig?" I cross my arms. "Thanks to you, there aren't going to be any more gigs."

"You're frickin' blind." Rozelle shakes her head. "This ain't no catastrophe. More like an op-por-tun-i-ty."

"What?" I explode. "How can you—?"

"You were the only one who took the Yo-Yo Prophet so seriously." She jabs a finger into my chest. "Everyone else knew it was just entertainment."

"I only took it seriously because you made me believe it was true."

"You needed to believe." Rozelle pushes her face close to mine. "It made you quit bein' a wuss."

I'm speechless. My face is hot. My fingers clench.

"Ha!" She points. "No comeback? You know I'm right! I beat the wuss outta you and gave you some spine. What's wrong with that?"

I can't think. Nothing makes sense. I step back.

The music stops abruptly. A tall lean guy with a shaved head squeezes into the doorway beside Rozelle. Although he's a couple of years older than her, they look so much alike that he has to be her brother.

"Roz, what's going on?" He examines my face. "Hey, I know you." He snaps his fingers. "Calvin, right? I'm Tyrone." He grips my hand and shakes. "You've been using my music in your shows. Thanks a lot, kid."

"S-sure, I stutter, trying to calm down.

Then he says, "I hear my sister's got you at the busker festival next weekend." He winks at Rozelle, who gets a proud tilt to her chin. "Things are going great for you."

My mouth drops open. "It's next weekend?" My head is spinning.

He laughs, deep and low. "You two need to talk." He elbows Rozelle aside. "You'd better come in."

Tyrone yanks me into the hall, past Rozelle, and into the kitchen, which is far from ghetto with its high-tech gas stove and stainless-steel fridge with an ice dispenser. Their parents must have some money, which is not what I imagined. Rozelle heads down the hall to the back of the house, and I wonder where she's going.

"Have a seat." Tyrone motions to a couple of stools pulled up to a marble counter. "Want a drink?"

"I'm not thirsty." I can't stop thinking about the busker festival next weekend. Could I perform again?

"Come on. It's the least I can do after you got me that exposure. You know, I'm getting more downloads than ever before. At this rate, maybe I'll get a recording contract before I'm fifty." He laughs.

"I didn't get you that exposure." I sit awkwardly. "Rozelle always talked about Teknonaut."

"Yeah, she says she hyped me big-time." He leans in close. "Tell me. Does my sister know the business as well as she thinks she does?"

"Don't tell her I said this, but sometimes I think she knows it too well."

"Yeah, she's done okay for you." Tyrone nods, hands me a can of Coke and then opens his own. "You know, she wants to build me a bigger profile, but I can't help wondering—what could my little sister know about it?"

He starts yakking about Rozelle's plans for him, while I'm remembering what Rozelle said when she first bullied her way into my business. *I gotta show my brother I can be a good manager.* Why didn't I see it before? It was all about Tyrone. She never cared about me.

"So what do you think of her?" Tyrone finally asks. "As a manager, I mean?"

I think carefully before I speak. "Rozelle would do anything to make me successful," I say. Even lie. "I can only imagine what she'd do for you."

Tyrone nods and strokes his chin. Rozelle meanders into the kitchen.

"Hey, sis," he calls. "Where were you?"

"Gettin' this." Rozelle slams her palm flat on the counter right in front of me.

I jump. "What are you doing?" That's when I see it. My neon yo-yo on the counter. Tyrone laughs. He sips his drink.

"Where did you find this?" I grab my yo-yo and examine the hairline crack along one rim.

Rozelle wanders to the fridge and grabs a root beer. "I got my ways." She pops open her can and takes a long swallow.

"Well, thanks." I pocket the yo-yo. She probably mowed some kid down to get it.

Rozelle leans against the counter and watches me. "I thought you might need it next weekend."

"Course he will." Tyrone guzzles the rest of his drink.

"I might." I nod slowly. Tyrone's enthusiasm makes me want to perform again, even though I'm terrified to face my pissed-off fans.

"Well, you two got things to talk about." Tyrone disappears into the hall, and the music starts up again.

With the techno beat thudding in my chest, I ask, "When am I supposed to perform?" I try to sound casual, like it doesn't matter much.

"Next Saturday. July twenty-third." Rozelle leans across the counter. "You gonna do it?"

"I think so."

"Huh!" She slurps her drink. "I figured you were too chicken."

I ignore her. "I just need to know where and when to show up. I'll handle this one myself." I tense up. "If they still want me."

"Why wouldn't they?" Rozelle gives me a careful look. Then she tells me the info. "Good luck, Yo-Yo," she says evenly, never taking her eyes off me.

"Thanks," I say. "But…you're not going to come, are you?" I hold my breath. Does she get what I'm saying? That I'll do this my way, without her?

Rozelle crushes her pop can and tosses it in a recycle bin next to the fridge. "Naw." She wipes her mouth and glances away. "You're better off without me. I'll just be in the way."

I narrow my eyes. What is she up to? "What about Sasha and Annette? Will they come?"

"Dunno. Ain't talked to 'em much."

I nod, relieved. The gang must have split up. I wonder if she's lonely. Not that I care. She did it to herself.

I leave Rozelle's place with the red Yo-Yo Prophet bucket in my hand and Tyrone's music running through my head. Outside, the clouds are clearing. A fresh breeze pushes me down the sidewalk, away from Rozelle.

I'm free of her. Finally. I swing the bucket and take big steps. I hope I can go it alone.

I take a different route out of Rozelle's neighborhood since I'm heading to the hospital to see Gran. On a quiet street, I see a homemade *For Rent* sign in front of a house.

I stop in my tracks. "No way."

The garden is weeds. The windows are grimy. It would look a lot like Rozelle's house, if it wasn't so run-down.

We'd be neighbors.

I stroll up the walk and ring the bell. Nothing happens. There are no curtains on the windows, so I push between the prickly bushes and peek in. Hardwood floors. Barren walls. No furniture.

I memorize the phone number.

As if anyone will rent to me.

I need an adult. Someone who knows about leases. Someone who—

"Spader!" I yelp.

I'm more worried before the busker festival than I was before my first show. And more confused too.

I faked being the Yo-Yo Prophet. Now, I'm not sure who I am—or what kind of show I should plan for the festival. They booked the Yo-Yo Prophet, but I don't fit the name anymore. I can yo-yo, but not like a master. And I'm a failed prophet. So what do I do? People will expect a prophet who can yo-yo, unless they've already heard about me—the prophet who can't predict the future.

I can do better than that. But how?

I ponder for days till I hit on a solution. *Entertainment and inspiration*, Rozelle once said. Entertainment I can give them. I'm not so sure about inspiration.

The rest of the week is a blur. I visit Gran twice a day, waiting for the results of her tests. Lucy and Franco come to see her as well—after Van tells them what happened—and they insist that one of them stays with me each night, which cramps my style, but keeps Family Services off my back. Spader sends Gran flowers, but my dad doesn't show up. I confirm my spot at the busker festival—they're still happy to have the Yo-Yo Prophet perform. I convince Spader to call about the house for rent near Rozelle's. I send Marshall an email, apologizing for lying to him. And I try to rehearse a performance like no other I've done before.

July 23 arrives faster than a street racer.

By eleven o'clock on Saturday morning, I'm weaving through the crowd at the busker festival, with my stomach doing flips. I'm wired with a headset supplied by the festival. It's attached to a battery pack clipped to the back of my shorts. My hair is spiked, still red at the tips. I'm even wearing the Yo-Yo Prophet T-shirt since I can't hide who I am, what I've done. Whether the crowd likes me or not, I'm here.

The buildings on Front Street trap the sun's heat between them. Barricades keep the cars off the roads. Crowds of people weave between the stalls of clothing for sale, food vendors, face painters and henna tattoo artists.

The racket from three nearby performers is deafening—clashing songs, miked voices and cheering hordes. I've got no music. No one to introduce me. Somehow, I'm supposed to set up a show for myself at an intersection of closed-off streets.

I squeeze past a kid playing a pennywhistle, people watching a beat-boxer, and a long lineup for souvlaki on a stick. As I inhale the scent of grilling pork, I let myself get jostled by the crowd.

Eventually I find the intersection where I'm supposed to perform. There are marks on the pavement for a wheelchair zone. People mill around me.

I wipe my sweaty hands on my shorts and unload my backpack. I've got a few surprises for my audience. I hope they won't hate the new Yo-Yo Prophet.

A roar erupts from the people watching the performer to the left of me. Over the heads of the crowd, I glimpse a man on stilts, juggling fiery torches.

Not bad. Better than a few yo-yo tricks from a guy accused of being a cheat and a liar. I swallow hard, push down the nervous rumblings in my stomach and plant myself a nice distance from the wheelchair zone.

This show's for Gran, I think. If she can fight to get better, I can face these people.

I turn on my mike. I set down my red Yo-Yo Prophet bucket. Then I fix my twin racers in place, one on each hand.

God, I miss Rozelle. She could call a crowd.

"Hey, folks," I say, getting a load of feedback from the mike. People wince and cover their ears.

I position the mike farther from my mouth, accidentally releasing a yo-yo. It falls and falters.

"Damn," I say into the mike.

A few parents glare. One man laughs. Maybe he thinks I'm a clown act.

A boy who looks about ten years old says, "Look, Mom. The Yo-Yo Prophet!" He's holding a blue yo-yo in his fist. "Can we stay?"

The mother nods. I've got my first two audience members.

I try to hold myself together.

"Welcome to the busker festival." I try not to think about how much better Rozelle would sound. "I'm Calvin Layne—the...uh...Yo-Yo Prophet."

No one boos. I start into my routine. A few simple yet impressive looping tricks. I turn in a slow circle, trying to pull people in.

A couple holding hands slows down briefly. A few kids sit cross-legged on the pavement, facing me.

I start blabbering, not sure what to say. "Two-handed yo-yoing mostly uses the forward pass." I perform a sample. "Around-the-world"—I swing into the trick with one yo-yo—"and loops." I return to two-handed loops.

A few people clap politely.

"Right now I'm tossing two-handed loops simultaneously." I change my rhythm. "But it's more fun to shoot one out while the other's coming back."

A middle-aged man in a red baseball cap stops to watch.

I shift my loops to vertical. "Vertical punches shoot the yo-yos straight up." I nod to the boy holding his yo-yo. "And here's a tip for this trick. You've got to keep your string tight and then punch hard. Make the yo-yo grab fast when it reaches the end of the string."

I'm rambling, trying to stay calm, trying to keep people interested.

I swing into inside loops combined with reach-for-the-moons. I've got a small group gathering in a circle. Maybe about twenty people, mostly kids. I notice a few people gripping yo-yos, but I don't have time to think about it. Because suddenly I hear familiar techno music booming. I glance sideways, almost losing my flow with the yo-yos. Rozelle is there, grinning sheepishly.

She swings the massive stereo off her shoulder with one arm. "Brought you some music," she shouts.

I can't believe I'm glad to see her. I can't believe she's demoted herself to volume control. "My sound technician is bringing us music from Tek-no-naut"—I pronounce it like Rozelle would—"an awesome new techno sound."

Rozelle gives me a sideways glance, but she doesn't object to her new job title, at least in front of the audience.

The music fuels my show. I pump my yo-yos in time to the beat. People catch the rhythm and hurl energy back at me. I pull into a looping arm wrap.

My crowd gets bigger, till it's an enormous circle of people. Kids sitting in front. Adults standing behind, craning their necks to see. Lots of teens too, which makes me jittery. It's my largest live audience ever. I couldn't escape if I wanted to.

I tug my yo-yos home. How many know about my failed predictions? Will my new show be enough to please them?

"Who wants to see some dawg racing?" I call into the mike.

A few people holler. I roll out a long piece of gray foam and set a few homemade cardboard ramps and moguls along it.

"Are you sure?" I'm buzzing with energy.

"Yeah!" They yell louder.

I get in position to throw out my yo-yos—one red racer and my battered neon yo-yo, with a new string. "Count down from three to start the race," I say. "Ready?"

The crowd cheers in reply. I glimpse two guys about my age, watching intently. Kids jump up and down. I start them off. "Four..."

"Three...two...one...go!" they shout.

"And they're off!" I walk-the-dog with both yo-yos, racing them along the foam. "Red is in front"—I'm talking like a sportscaster—"but neon is catching up." I run my dogs over a ramp. "Who's going to win?"

Some people call out.

"Red's winning!" a girl yells.

"Go, neon!" shouts the man in the baseball cap. He seems pretty keen.

Tyrone's music gets intense, pounding out a wacky sequence of notes. My dogs speed over the moguls. Red is still in front.

"One final ramp!" I bellow.

The two yo-yos battle for position. They head into the last, and biggest, ramp. Red topples sideways. Neon jumps the ramp, landing neatly at the end of the foam.

The crowd laughs and cheers. I'm flying.

"Neon wins!" I raise my arms.

Someone calls from behind. "How about a prediction, Yo-Yo Prophet?" There's something nasty about his voice.

I spin around, catching my breath, trying not to panic.

There's a man with silver hair and a jeering smile. He's standing near the back, but he's tall enough to see over people's heads.

"This kid's been giving fake predictions all summer." The man scoffs. "I saw it on TV."

"I…uh…" I choke on my words. The music throbs. Sweat beads on my forehead.

"I heard it too." It's a woman with huge sunglasses and painted pink lips.

The crowd hums with conversation.

"Is it true?"

"Sure is."

"He's just a kid."

"What a loser."

My throat goes dry. They'll boo me out of the festival.

Rozelle steps into the circle. "What Calvin is tryin' to say is that it ain't his fault. If you gotta blame someone, blame me. I was his manager, till he fired me. He knew nothin' 'bout the false predictions."

I stare at Rozelle. She's taking the fall for me? Then I get it. She'll do anything for my success—even destroy her reputation. God, she's good.

"What—is he stupid?" the man taunts. "He had to know!"

Rozelle shakes her head. "Me and my girls—we did it all. Believe it or don't."

I watch Rozelle in action. Some adults are frowning. The two guys my age are smirking. Most of the kids are staring wide-eyed and eager, some of them clutching yo-yos.

I can't let her efforts go to waste.

"I'll give you a prediction, but I'll need a volunteer." I shoot a look at Rozelle, hoping someone in the crowd will go for it. "Who wants to come up here and learn a trick?"

Hands shoot up all over the audience. Rozelle melts back beside the music box. I pick the boy who first stopped to watch. The one with the blue yo-yo. He's got short blond hair and eyes that are too close together. He tells me his name is Zack.

I signal Rozelle to turn down the music. "Do you know how to walk-the-dog?" I ask Zack.

"No." His voice is high-pitched and quiet. His eyes sweep the mob nervously.

"Today, you're going to learn." I position him at one end of the foam and then instruct him in the basics of the trick. "You got it?"

"I guess." His forehead furrows.

I put a hand on his shoulder and try to sound confident, even though my legs are shaking. "I predict you're going to ace this trick," I say into the mike.

A murmur runs through the crowd.

Zack's brown eyes shine. "Okay."

I give Zack a few pointers. "Go for it." I smile. It feels good to help him believe in himself. I glance at Rozelle. Maybe she wasn't so bad—some of the time.

After a false start, Zack walks-the-dog down to the first ramp. Not quite an accurate prediction, but Zack is happy.

The crowd applauds him.

"Awesome job!" I clap too. "Will you help me with another trick?"

"Yeah." He's louder now.

I pull out three soft foam balls. They're bright yellow and smaller than tennis balls.

"Throw these one at a time in front of me—around shoulder height—when I shout 'Pull.' Got it?"

"Sure." He beams.

"Great!" I say. "It's time for some skeet shooting!"

The audience cheers.

I start looping with both my twin racers. "I predict I'll hit the first ball and the third ball with one of my yo-yos," I call into the mike, not caring if I'm accurate. I can't pretend to be someone I'm not.

Once I'm channeling the power of my twin racers, I bellow, "Pull!"

Zack throws the first ball. I hit it. The crowd roars.

A little girl catches the ball and rolls it back to Zack.

"Lucky guess!" yells the heckler.

"Pull," I shout again, ignoring him.

I hit it again. People groan, like they're sorry for me.

"Too bad. Maybe I'll get the next prediction right." I grin. "Pull."

I smash the third one. The crowd goes crazy. They drown out the heckler, who scowls and then turns away.

"Thanks so much," I holler over the applause. I'm floating ten feet off the ground.

Zack returns to his mother, beaming.

The crowd is pumped.

I flip the balls and one of my racers to my backpack. I jump into position for my final sequence of tricks.

"Now for my grand finale." I bow as the crowd shouts for more. "But first, I want to say that if you liked what you saw, please toss a few coins or bills my way after the show." I motion to my red bucket. "And you should know"—I take a breath—"that I'm donating all the money from today's performance to East General Hospital, where my grandmother is a patient." I pause. "This is for you, Gran," I say.

There's silence. Did I blow it? Then a burst of applause. I grin. Rozelle blasts the music. I launch into the routine I've been practicing for days.

First, I blaze through all the tricks I've mastered. A double or nothing. Three-leaf clover. Skin-the-cat. Atomic bomb. It's so satisfying. My shoulders are loose. I'm in the rhythm.

Rozelle starts a chant. "Cal-vin! Cal-vin!" It's good to hear my own name. When others pick it up, I can't help smiling.

Next, I fire the big guns. Buddha's revenge. Zipper. Shockwave. Cold fusion. Even a double iron whip.

I don't distinguish faces anymore. I hardly hear the crowd. I exist alone, with my yo-yo.

I finish with a perfect Yuuki slack.

The crowd erupts into a riot of screaming.

I feel dizzy, energized. I wave and bow. "Thank you!"

I don't have to beat Black Magic to win.

My bucket overflows with money. Coins litter the asphalt.

People swarm me, saying how much they liked the show. I demonstrate a few moves for Zack and some other eager yo-yoers. I notice the man in the red baseball cap hanging around. A few people have brought their own yo-yos. Rozelle saunters over as the mob eases.

"The yo-yo geeks are out in full force today." She grins.

"Yeah, I didn't know there were so many of us around."

"It's a frickin' epidemic. They love you." She slaps my back, but not hard enough to knock me over.

"Thanks, Rozelle." I smile.

"It was nothin'." She glances away. "I owed ya."

That's a first. "What for?"

"My brother. I dunno what you said to him, but he's finally lettin' me be his manager."

"Really? That's great. But I didn't do much."

"Whatever." She shrugs. "Anyway, I gotta retire from bein' your manager. I got big plans for Tyrone, so no beggin' me to stay."

Who's begging? "What about Sasha and Annette? Marshall?"

"What 'bout 'em?"

"Are they going to help?"

"Naw. They're too pissed off."

"Too bad."

"They'll get over it. And if they don't, they miss out."

I nod. "I guess you're right."

Rozelle takes off. I shove my gear into my backpack. I wonder if I should warn Tyrone about Rozelle—explain how far she's willing to go for her "talent." But he must know what she's like. Maybe that's why he was hesitating. As I'm picking up the last few coins off the asphalt, I hear a voice.

"Calvin Layne? Do you have a minute?"

I turn to see the guy in the baseball cap. "Sure." I nod.

"Great!" He holds out his hand. "I'm Dennis Harley. I run a gaming and collectibles store on Bloor Street, and I have a business proposition for you."

On August 1, I'm carrying a cardboard box into our newly rented house—the one near Rozelle's. The garden is still full of weeds and the windows are still grimy, but I've never seen a more beautiful sight.

My shoulders ache as I cross the creaky wooden porch. I have no idea what's in the box since I forgot to label it, but it's heavy enough to be Gran's royal china. I step carefully, squeezing sideways through the doorway. Inside, it smells like lemon-scented cleaner and leftover pizza—a powerful combination. I dump the box in the living room and then rub my shoulders.

"Good news, Calvin," Van calls, her voice echoing off the hardwood floor and the bare walls. Van's granddaughter,

Misha, was born about a week ago, and she's already at home with her mother. I'm glad Van is here, even if it is only for a visit.

"What happened?" I meander over to the front windows, where Van is attacking the grime with a bucket of soapy water and a cloth.

"My daughter called." She waves toward the telephone sitting in a dusty corner. "She says Misha smiled for the first time when Samuel was singing to her, although I suspect Misha may have just had gas. Either way, she is doing well."

"That's great." I grin. "I bet you can't wait to get back to them."

"Yes, but first there is work to be done here. So much dirt!" She rinses her cloth.

"Thanks, Van." I know the place will be spotless before she leaves.

"What you standin' 'round for?" Rozelle clomps into the room, peering over the two large boxes she is carrying. "You expect me to do all your work?" She unloads her boxes next to mine.

"Who made you boss?" I fake a punch to her gut.

Rozelle catches my fist easily. "Remind me to teach ya how to fight." She smirks.

It takes most of the afternoon to empty the truck that Van rented. As I haul boxes with Rozelle, I think about how random life can be. I mean, if I hadn't met Rozelle, I wouldn't have become the Yo-Yo Prophet. If Gran hadn't opened a dry-cleaning shop, she wouldn't be sick. My parents wouldn't have met. I wouldn't even exist. Which only proves how impossible it is to predict what will happen next. Just when I think I have everything figured out, there's a new trick to master.

As we're finishing, Spader appears with some last-minute papers for Gran to sign—something about the renter's insurance he's insisting we get.

With his long arms and legs, he reminds me of a grasshopper. He hands me the papers, along with a stack of letters. "You need to forward your mail," he tells me. "Get your grandmother to do it, when she can."

"I will." I walk him to the door and say goodbye, glad to be rid of him. He's been helpful, but I still don't like him that much.

Looking through the stack of mail, which has been building up for a while, I notice a letter from my school. My report card. I tear it open, hoping my math mark isn't too terrible.

"I got a C in math," I tell Van. It's not a B, like I predicted, but it'll do.

"Is that all?" Rozelle comes up behind me. She reads over my shoulder. "I got a B."

“No way!” I turn, holding my report against my chest. “You hardly went to class!”

“You callin’ me a liar?” Rozelle takes a step closer. She breathes in my face.

“No.” I snort. “I know how smart you are.”

“Damn right.” Rozelle nods, satisfied.

Van and I give Rozelle a ride home. After we drop off the truck, we head to the hospital to visit Gran.

I plan to tell Gran more about the house—where she can plant a garden, where she can hang her collection of royal plates, which bedroom I claimed. Dr. Chen has said she can leave the hospital once we make arrangements for home care. At least I’ll have some help after Van leaves.

As we enter Gran’s room, I’m relieved to see her sitting up in bed, talking on the phone. She’s got a new nightgown on—a blue one that Van brought. Her eyes are bright as she waves us in. Although she’s lost a lot of weight, it’s the best I’ve seen her in months.

“Yes, I got your gift basket,” she says into the phone, pointing at a shrink-wrapped basket filled with gourmet teas and English biscuits. *From Richard*, she mouths.

My jaw drops. I glance at Van, whose eyes are wide.

“Calvin told you that?” Gran’s eyes find mine. “He’s been under a great deal of stress.”

No kidding. I hurry to the basket and check the card. *Richard*, it reads. I stiffen. He's never sent anything before. What does it mean?

"No, I'm cancer free, apparently." Gran stifles a small cough. "They can't explain the pain in my kidneys, but it could be much worse. I could be heading into chemotherapy." She pauses to listen.

I strain to hear his voice through the phone. Van steps out into the hall and shuts the door, probably to give us privacy.

"Yes, I remember." Gran's voice softens. She shudders.

Remember what? My mother?

"He's here. Just a minute." Gran holds the phone out. "He's asking for you."

"Me?" I take the phone, cautiously, like it might burn my hand, and put the receiver to my ear. "Hello?"

"I...uh"—my father's voice is gravelly—"got your messages, son."

"Yeah?" I nod. "You could have called." The word *son* bothers me. He's hardly been a father.

"Yes, well, I wanted to say that...I'm...sorry I missed your calls."

"Sure." I clench my jaw. Time for the violins to play. Time for him to say that he never meant to hurt me.

That he'll be home soon. That he was just too busy. That he lost his cell. Whatever.

He blathers on. "I told your grandmother that I can't travel right now. I'm tied up with this show..."

I stop listening. I don't need him to come. He doesn't belong here anymore. He hasn't for a long time. Even though it'll be hard, we can do it ourselves.

"It's okay," I interrupt. "You don't need to leave work. Gran is much better, and we've got a great place to live. Listen, I've got to go, but you can call later at our new number." I tell him the number. Then I hang up.

Gran gives me a funny smile. "What was that about?"

I shrug. "We'll be fine without him." I squeeze her hand. He's let us both down, again and again, but at least we have each other.

Van and I visit with Gran for a few hours and grab some supper at the cafeteria. Afterward, I take the subway to my new job.

Game Z—Dennis Harley's store—stands at the corner of two busy streets in the west end. He sells video games, retro board games, every action figure you can imagine, gaming books and even a few comic books. It may be one of the coolest stores I've ever seen. In the window is a poster-sized photo of my grinning face.

Yo-Yo Master Calvin Layne, it announces in huge red letters on a yellow background. *Appearing weekly*. I love seeing my real name in print.

At the busker festival, Dennis told me how his grandfather used to tour for a big yo-yo manufacturer back in the thirties, performing and teaching tricks. "Sounds like a dream job," I said. Then Dennis offered me this gig.

A tune from a movie soundtrack plays when I open the door. Inside by the front cash, there's a wall-to-wall yo-yo display with tons of models: butterfly and classic, beginner and expert, glow-in-the-dark and off-string. I've bought a Silver Bullet already—the selection is as good as my favorite online shop.

Dennis is behind the counter. His freckled face brightens when he looks up. "There's a bigger group today." He bounces out to greet me. "Mostly twelve-year-olds and teens, and one guy about thirty. Word travels fast."

"Great." I pull out my new Silver Bullet—I've retired my neon one—and shove my backpack behind the counter.

From the rear of the store comes the sound of excited voices.

"Calvin Layne's here!"

"I see him!"

I shoot Dennis a lopsided smile.

"Oh, yeah." Dennis snaps his fingers. "There's a guy back there who says he knows you. Someone from school? His name is Geordie."

"He came here?" I grin. Of course Geordie would know this store. Maybe we can hang out afterward. I head for the back.

"Who wants to reach-for-the-moon?" I call.

A cheer erupts.

I toss out my yo-yo and show them how it's done.

ACKNOWLEDGMENTS

During the writing of this book, the Ontario Arts Council and the City of Toronto through the Toronto Arts Council generously provided financial support. Pat Bourke, Patricia McCowan, Karen Rankin and Sarah Raymond offered astute critiques on the work-in-progress. Members of the forums at yoyonation.com and yoyoexpert.com demonstrated and explained yo-yo tricks. Barb Thompson generously answered my medical queries. Sarah Harvey and the team at Orca Books provided insightful editorial and production support. My family listened to me rant about yo-yo performances and praised my wobbly yo-yo tricks. Thanks to all for your support.

KAREN KROSSING is addicted to stories. She began to create her own stories when she was eight, and today she writes novels and short stories for children and teens. Karen also encourages new writers through workshops for kids, teens and adults. Karen lives with her family in Toronto, Ontario, where she volunteers at a family shelter and practices her yo-yo tricks. *The Yo-Yo Prophet* is her first book with Orca. For more about Karen, please visit karenkrossing.com.